I0584820

# ORBITAL PREY

# ORBITAL PREY

## HUNTERS OF SORASK - 1

## BY MATT PARSONS

Copyright © 2025 by Matt Parsons

All rights reserved. No part of this publication may be reproduced, stored in a retrieval system, or transmitted in any form or by any means—electronic, mechanical, photocopying, recording, or otherwise—without the prior written permission of the copyright owner.

This novel is a work of fiction. Names, characters, places, and incidents are either the product of the author's imagination or used fictitiously. Any resemblance to actual persons, living or dead, events, or locales is entirely coincidental.

ISBN: 979-8-9993238-0-4 (Paperback)
ISBN: 978-1-234567-89-1 (eBook)

Cover art by Pantelis
Interior illustrations by Inkerclark
Book layout by Keven Albers

First Edition

# PROLOGUE

A SPACER LEARNS what fear is the day he finds the empty vacuum of space is not as empty as it should be.

Faldos thought he knew fear. He thought fear was staring out the mouth of the shuttle bay and seeing no stars. He thought it came from the knowledge that outside the survey ship's rusty hull, was a lightless field of pitch-black metallic shards.

The dredgers called it the Obsidian Shroud. Faldos called it unnerving.

Even a mid-sized survey ship like the *Scavenging Savant* was dwarfed by the larger shards. Like a bug under a boulder. But actually the bigger concern was the volume of smaller shards, finer than sand that smothered radio signals from entering or leaving. Faldos' eyes followed the ship's searchlights, golden beams that struggled to cut through the billowing black dust.

In the gloom, Faldos imagined Voidforms or Leviathans lurking just beyond the light's rays. Out here, nobody would ever know what happened. The *Scavenging Savant* would be just one more missing starship in the Shroud.

*Could've been a waystation fry cook,* Faldos thought.

Granted, Voidforms were myths and Leviathans were all but extinct. Yet knowing that didn't stop Faldos' mind from working shadows into nightmares. He told himself such terrors were for children.

This irrational, childish tension in his gut, he believed, was fear.

But it was not.

The searchlights settled on a colossal black shard. A mountain in the void. This shard was their target. Their meal ticket.

The Obsidian Shroud was a place of darkness. Of isolation. But also of potential fortune.

Those aboard the *Scavenging Savant* dredged the Obsidian Shroud for one material: kuron.

Technically, it was all around them. But in small and mixed quantities. And unfortunately, finding purer kuron required a closer look.

"Riches await," Faldos said, swallowing a throat as dry as the void. He pulled out his controller, fiddling with presets. "Again we reach out into the void for a couple coins. Then it's eat slop, rest on a lumpy bed and do it all again tomorrow. I wouldn't trade it for all the worlds. How about you?"

A skeletal form stood beside him. Six spindly arms and two legs, all held together by metal strings. Some hands ended in clawed fingers, others in machines. The single eye in its metal skull was blank and lifeless.

The puppet's name was Ardor and it was the closest thing Faldos had to a friend onboard. Even then it only stuck around because he held its strings.

"We're both on strings," Faldos mused. "But you don't mind yours, right? Must be nice to have a puppeteer of such status and stature as me." Faldos stretched himself up to his measly peak height and flexed all six arms.

Ardor didn't reply. He was a puppet.

Faldos sighed, dropping his arms limply. He didn't fool himself either.

The two of them were bathed in the burnt orange light of the ship's nearby core. Due to the cramped nature of the vessel, the shuttle bay, cargo hold and engineering deck were all one shared compartment.

The core, a glowing sphere suspended by piping, with veiny wires splitting off it, was clutched by the withered roots of the ship's tree. The tree was equal parts small and gnarled, and should have been replaced years ago. It never had due to cost, like many things on the *Scavenging Savant*. As a result, they needed supplemental oxygen recyclers and were also prone to the occasional radiation leak.

Faldos wondered how many years of his life this ship was taking off him. But even this thought didn't make him eager to leave it for the murky void outside.

"What's taking so long, stringer?" Captain Froll said over the radio. The gravelly voice was as unpleasant as the man himself. "I'm not paying ya to stargaze!"

"Sorry, sir. I got held up putting my suit on."

"What d'ya need that for? We've got a breathing barrier."

"I guess I was just wondering how much I trust this rusty can of a ship and its appliances to protect me outside of a pressurized hull."

"Well, you've got your suit on now, what's holding you up still?"

"Are you sure Daley can't do it? He's more experienced."

"I told ya, he's too drunk to walk in a straight line, now you want the commission for that rock, or what?"

"I do."

"I do?"

"I do...sir."

"Good. Then be a star and get out there before I have Breff throw ya out."

Breff, the wide-bellied and furry Simacha engineer standing nearby, sized him up and shrugged as if it would be a simple undertaking. Faldos grinned like that was a joke, though in truth he wasn't sure.

"R-roger that, Captain."

A single cable dangled from Ardor's back, to the controller held in Faldos' own six hands. He flipped a switch, bringing Ardor to life. Its single eye glowed red.

Faldos pulled on six different analog sticks at once, tilting them in different directions. In response, Ardor stretched its limbs, wire muscle fibers extending to their limits. Faldos released the sticks and the puppet relaxed. Everything seemed functional.

"Let's get to work, buddy," Faldos said. "Otherwise the boss might *string* us up."

Ardor didn't laugh. He was a puppet.

The two of them inched up to the bay mouth.

"Bridge, you mind dropping gravity for me?" Faldos said into his cuff.

The ship's artificial gravity flipped off, and Ardor and Faldos floated freely. Handholds popped out of Ardor's back. Faldos grabbed onto four of the handholds, keeping his remaining two hands on the puppet's controller. He hesitated from going further.

*Sometimes you gotta do something you hate so you don't hate yourself.* Words of Faldos' father. Often used to get his son to do chores. Some days the phrase seemed to be the only thing keeping Faldos going. His father probably would have loved this kind of work.

Faldos punched the thrusters. Gas erupted from the puppet's feet. They sped away from the safety of the ship's Kuron alloy hull. Waiting above, orbiting the main body of the starship, was the satellite ring. It bristled with searchlights, sensors and other tools.

In the space between, they traveled through the medium of the ship's breathing barrier. Air was projected so space suits were unnecessary to work outside the hull. Faldos always wore one anyway. He could almost imagine his father springing out here without so much as a shirt.

Each meter brought Faldos and Ardor closer to the edge of the artificial atmosphere. And each moment the ebbs and flows of the black tide attacked the ship, washing it with waves of shards. Too small and too fast, these shards flashed and splintered into pale motes, and then nothing. At least the ship's ashfield worked.

Faldos pulled Ardor to a stop as they reached the satellite ring. He lowered himself from the puppet, his boots sealing onto the metal.

Here he stood at the shoreline of the Shroud. A few rocky shards came close, almost touching Faldos before they burned to ash.

*Nothing out here but rocks,* he thought, incorrectly.

A large winch waited for them, bolted to the ring. Faldos unhooked his controller cable from Ardor's back. Its eyelight blinked that it was without command. He pulled out a length of the winch's cable and plugged that into the puppet's back instead. He then plugged his controller into the winch's console, re-establishing a connection to the puppet.

The interference out here made radio control unreliable so they had to rely on hardlines. He'd argued for them to connect the hardline all the way down to the bridge, so he could tie in inside of the ship. There should've been one already, if not for the ship's shoddy wiring. But the captain insisted that it was better this way. If anything went wrong and the puppet got damaged or stuck, he could quickly retrieve it. The thought made Faldos shiver.

He fired the puppet's thrusters again, sending it deeper into the void, the winch spitting out cable as it went. The puppet cut through the flow of rocky dust, sending out ripples of collisions. The shards of the old moons were all-encompassing.

Faldos' target, the gargantuan shard of debris, sat a little over two hundred meters away. They had several times that length in cable, so that wasn't a concern. Still, it might take a minute; plowing through the debris at full speed would wear down Ardor's armor.

"Is your puppet still not in place yet?" the captain's voice barked in Faldos' ear.

"Almost, sir."

"You realize you don't get paid by the hour, right?"

"I get paid?"

"Keep trying to be funny, no one's laughing. And no, you don't get paid, not if you don't find us any kuron."

Training to be a space-based structural engineer, Faldos had imagined himself designing colonial megastructures and orbital habitats. Turns out they didn't need that many designers for mega-structures.

Ardor reached the shard, two arms shooting spikes down to grip hold of it. Next, another hand shot a laser into the body of the rock. A readout of the constituent elements showed up on Faldos' display, values shifting as the laser bored deeper.

"Only low purity kuron so far," Faldos reported. "But I'll keep digging."

"There was some kind of cavity on the other side when it rotated earlier. Check in there, might give you a closer look at the center."

"Understood and underway." He moved Ardor further along the rockface, rounding the bend and passing out of Faldos' view. He switched to Ardor's camera view, graced with the idyllic vista…of more black rock. It wasn't long before he found the cavity the captain mentioned. It started out as a wide depression, but quickly funneled down into a lightless cavern. Faldos moved Ardor inside and switched the puppet's lights on. The beams didn't penetrate far, dust fogging the view.

As Ardor descended the gloom swallowed him. The cable scraped against the edge, sending vibrations all the way down to the winch beside Faldos.

At length, Ardor found the bottom, just more featureless black rock.

"Reached the bottom of the cavity, starting analysis."

The laser fired again.

"Whoa," Faldos said.

"What is it?"

"Almost ninety percent kuron content. Laser's barely scratching the surface."

"Spread out, see if it's just a fluke."

"Already on it."

Lasers on Ardor's other arms cut across the cavity, targeting different points, all while keeping the first engaged.

"We're doing great! There's minor variations in the values, but all of them are steady around eighty-nine percent kuron."

"Now that calls for a round of drinks! Still, keep at it for the next hour or so, I don't want to find out it's nothing more than a lining."

"Typical," Faldos muttered.

"What was that?"

"I mean uh, acknowledged...sir."

"That's right."

The captain aside, Faldos found his mood improving. They'd struck big on this one. Maybe the commission would even be enough to get away from this-

Something moved on the edge of Ardor's field of view. Faldos jerked the puppet around but the light hit nothing but floating rocks.

*Jumping at shadows,* he told himself.

*One hundred percent kuron.* Faldos blinked. The laser's value dropped back down seconds later. There was no way that in an unrefined shard of a broken moon, there would be a one-hundred percent pure kuron reading. Faldos checked the log. The distance of the beam's reflection had changed too. Meaning something had passed in between the laser and the cavern wall.

Faldos felt a cold chill cut down his spine. He was reminded of reports of other survey vessels going missing. But surely that'd just been due to poor navigation of the debris field...right?

He rotated Ardor slowly, turning both his searchlight and the lasers, going for maximum coverage of the cavern.

*One-hundred percent kuron.* He whirled Ardor around to follow the laser. He caught sight of a shadowy form as it passed out of view, laser value dropping down again.

"...captain," Faldos's voice cracked.

"What is it? Don't tell me it was just an outer layer?"

"No it's...there's something down there with Ardor. Something moving."

"What is it? Another puppet? Don't tell me some other survey ship's staked claim."

Another puppet. Of course. It made sense. Building puppets out of kuron was rare, but not unheard of. Although, Faldos hadn't seen another cable when he entered the cavity. It must have come down after them. Though…they hadn't detected another ship approaching. But with so much kuron ore dust around, sensors were hardly reliable. It was almost a reasonable explanation.

Almost.

"Do me a favor and smash the other puppet if you find him," the captain said.

So barbaric. But Faldos did continue his search. He wasn't about to cede a paycheck this big to some other survey crew. If things got rough then so be—

*One-hundred percent kuron.* This time from two different lasers, almost twenty meters between the two points of interruption. It dropped off one, and shortly after, the other.

That…would have to be one large puppet.

It passed through another two lasers-no, three. His first thought was that it was even bigger than expected, but that wasn't the main reason.

It was getting closer.

Faldos whipped Ardor around once more, searchlight blazing. He finally saw something, but only a glimpse. Something large and dark. A small and thin part of it coiled, then struck Ardor, sending the puppet spinning.

The puppet's head struck ore, smashing the camera. The video feed went dead.

It was time to go.

Faldos hit the retractor on the winch. He was getting his puppet out of here. And himself for that matter.

"Captain, I don't know what's down there but I don't think it's another puppet. We need to get out of here, right now!"

"What are you on about now? I'm not about to give up a chunk of high purity kuron just because you're jumping at—"

"You aren't listening! It's some kind of…of…"

*Of what?*

Ardor's ascent jerked to a stop. A violent tremble shook the winch's cable. Ardor had gotten caught on something. Or…something had grabbed onto Ardor. Faldos fired the puppet's thrusters. The puppet remained in place.

Faldos cranked the winch to reel in at full force. The motor whined, but Ardor didn't move.

He pointed all of Ardor's lasers below and cranked the intensity to max. But the lasers struck pure kuron. Like trying to carve diamonds with a plastic knife.

It, whatever it was, started pulling Ardor back down towards the bottom of the cavity. The winch screeched in pain as it was forcibly relieved of a few meters of cable.

*Come on,* Faldos urged. *You can make it, Ardor.*

As if spurned by his silent call, the cable jerked sharply, and the reel resumed its mad retraction. First confused, Faldos found his answer on the controller's readout.

Ardor's legs were nonexistent. Ripped apart by the dual forces of the winch and whatever clutched him.

Ardor hit the edge of the cavern on his way out, sending trembles up the cable. The controller howled damage alarms as the puppet bumped along the rock.

Ardor rounded the bend and came into view of Faldos' natural eyes. The puppet finally parted from the shard, battered armor as a souvenir.

A shadow followed.

Faldos could discern little but the general shape. It was large and wide, with no rounded edges to it. All components were sharp. As if the swords of a hundred giants had half melted into a single, terrible weapon.

Very late, did Faldos fully recall that he was no longer separated by the barrier of a screen. He stood exposed on the outer rim of the ship's satellite ring. He should've moved then. But his legs were solid as stone.

The shadow didn't trail behind Ardor for long. Instead, it swept back and forth in wide arcs that slowly brought it ever closer to the ship. Ripples of rocky debris pushed out ahead of it with each sweep. It passed in and out of the ship's searchlight beams, none capturing the complete image of it.

"Are you still reeling your puppet in?" the captain's voice barked.

"I swear if we lose this haul, you'll be missing more than just a job when this is over!"

The captain's horrible grating voice was what finally broke Faldos from his immobile staring.

He didn't speak. He instead shared a live feed of his helmet's cam with the captain. Looking at it now, he saw that the impression of fused swords was flawed. This thing was more akin to the shards surrounding them. As if a piece of the Obsidian Shroud had come to life to put an end to the intruders of its realm.

When the captain could speak, he swore. "...ash it all...is that another ship?"

"Doesn't really look like any ship I've seen."

The captain cleared his throat. "Well, it'll take more than that to spook Captain-"

A thin extension of the shadow split out from the main body, reaching out to mingle with a shard the size of a small shuttle. It flicked like a whip and sent the shard rocketing towards them. Most of it was shredded by the ship's protective ashfield. A small dark piece still grazed the satellite ring before that too flared and faded.

"...ash this, we're getting out of here!" the captain shouted.

The orange glow of the ship's main thruster blazed to life. The aging engine was warming up. It'd be a minute before they started moving. A minute suddenly seemed so very long.

Faldos shot one last look at Ardor and the shadow behind it. It might've been the best puppet he'd ever used, but Faldos wasn't about to get killed for it. There was a chance it was close enough to radio control. All he could do was key in a few instructions for Ardor to follow, and hope for the best. He disconnected the controller, turned around, and jumped for it.

He seemed to drift back to the cargo bay with aching slowness. So exposed, so vulnerable. What if the ship's thrusters engaged while he was still hanging in empty space, and he was left behind with that...thing?

But he slammed into the unforgiving metal of the cargo bay without incident. Immediately the bay door began to shut.

Ardor reached the end of the winch and automatically disconnected, the momentum carrying it forward. Per instructions, Ardor's
secondary thrusters on his back gave him a final push. At the same
time, the ship's engines pulsed and the ship began to move forward,
though not yet at full tilt.

One of the sudden movements, either the puppet's acceleration
or the ship's—Faldos didn't know which—spurred the shadow to
chase.

A dull flare of orange in the dark, and the shadow shot forward.

Ardor slipped between the doors a moment before they slammed
shut. The puppet crashed across the floor and slid beside him. Faldos
let out a breath he hadn't realized he was holding.

"Wh...what was that?" Breff the engineer asked, stumbling forward.

Faldos shook his head. "I don't know, but I'm glad we're leaving
it behi—"

It slammed into the ship.

They felt little impact, the inertial dampeners would take care
of that.

Instead, there was the almost vibration-less impact of a large
section of hull buckling inward.

Despite feeling almost nothing, Faldos nearly fell over.

Breff's eyes bulged. "Th-that's impossible. That hull is a Kuron
alloy."

There was a second impact, driving the dent deeper, and this
time there was a slight tremor the inertial dampeners couldn't quite
smother.

"It...doesn't seem to care," Faldos found himself saying.

He shared a look with Breff.

"The bridge?"

"I sure ain't stayin' here!"

They sprinted away as the third impact landed. The stairs leading
up to the bridge were taken three at a time.

Through a hatch they found the captain barking orders at the frazzled helmsman and deck operators. Captain Froll was a Simacha too, equally furry as Breff but nearly as wiry as Faldos. His tail twitched in furious anxiety.

The Shroud roiled outside. Shards crashed into one another and tumbled into the ship. Many were ashed but a disturbing number were slipping through to make impact. The inertial dampener ate most of these impacts. But dull tremors were starting to carry through.

"What's happening?" Faldos asked.

"The other ship—gotta be another ship—she's crafty. Real crafty." The captain rambled. "Making shards crash into us. We've lost most of our exterior cameras and now got no visuals on her. Think I can track her thrusters, though…"

A holographic projection tracked a faint orange glow through the gloom.

"There you are…"

The projection showed the ship's satellite ring spin up an illsur drill, charged with ashen energy. It pivoted towards the approaching shadow. There was a jerk of motion and the ring spun away.

The snapped off drill flew past the bridge's porthole.

"Uh…"

"Full speed?" the helmsman asked.

"Full speed!"

The ship's thrusters blasted and they tore away from the other glow. The helmsman whipped them between the largest shards. The smaller ones, battling the ashfield, continued to rack up impacts across the hull. Faldos' hands instinctively found a wall to brace himself against. On the holo projection, the other glow slowly fell behind them.

Faldos and everyone else let out a sigh of relief.

The glow behind brightened and started catching up.

"Faster…" the captain said.

"We're already at full burn!" the helmsman cried.

The glow was nearing. The captain sent the ring back to swing another drill at the approaching entity. Another drill broke. Shortly after, the systems warned that a section of the ring had been ripped clean off.

A second later it reached the ship. The whole vessel lurched.

"Taking on more mass!" one of the operators reported. "Acceleration slowing marginally."

"She's got us hooked somehow. We'll just shake 'em!"

They started zigzagging the ship, cutting through streams of black debris. One curve was misjudged, and the ship slammed into the side of a shard five times its size. The ashfield flared with blinding light, softening their area of impact, then fell dead.

"We just lost the ashfield!"

"We'll deal with it later, get us out of here!"

The ship started accelerating again. They plunged through a storm of shards, raining down on the ship like hailstones. Unprotected by ashfield, the shards pockmarked the front of the ship, one cracking the viewport.

The other glow started up again too.

The diagram indicated it was now twisting towards the opposite direction.

"Acceleration slowing dramatically!"

"She's dragging us!"

"Taking minor hull damage from the bow! Engaging blast shields!"

A metal plate slid over the viewport, and they were now seeing exclusively by hologram.

"Damage on the stern!" another operator reported.

The orange glow flared again and the sound of metal grinding rang out from the other end of the ship.

"Stern hull damage is increasing!"

"Acceleration approaching nil!"

In the face of this tugging match with a thing that was not a ship, Faldos felt himself growing distant from the events around him. As if he were a mere observer, watching through his controller's screen.

What was this feeling?

A scream, the tearing of metal further in the ship, but not far enough, made it all so clear.

Fear. It held him still like the strings of a puppet.

Then, under the many trembling forces upon the Scavenging Savant, a pipe burst, just above. Flinching away from the scalding vapor, he slipped and hit the metal face first. Even with his suit on, his brain still took a rattling.

Once on the floor he didn't much care to get up.

But somewhere in that cranial trauma a memory was knocked loose.

He'd been climbing the wires on the Stitched Chasm, when one broke. The fall, in retrospect, would not have been so great, ten meters at the most to the platform below. But it'd seemed a kilometer with the wind threatening to break his grip. So, he'd locked up for the better part of an hour until his father found him and dragged him up.

*"You know, Faldos, I won't always be there. Someday you gotta grab your own strings and pull for dear life."*

His father was indeed not here anymore. And here he was again, dangling over an abyss. Was he still too scared to try and climb to the top?

As he sat back and took in the rusty, grease coated ship that was about to be torn to shreds, he learned something about himself.

He wasn't ready to die. Not in this place. Not for this job. Not for this pay.

All six of Faldos' hands squeezed into fists.

Faldos grabbed hold of those strings of fear and pulled hard. He sprang to his feet, lucidity rushing into him like a shot of ice into his veins.

"Breff!" Faldos barked. "You know this ship's engine better than anyone, can we get some kind of boost? Lose weight by dropping some cargo? Anything?"

"We're already at full tilt, that's everything she's got. Dumping cargo won't help if we're hooked. There's not much we can do, unless..."

"Unless?"

"Agh, they always tell ya never to do this…but we could plunge the core into the fuel reservoir. The shock of the reaction will blow the core, but it'll give us one Sunder of a boost for a second. Might break their hold on us."

"Let's do that!"

"But there are safeguards! You'd melt your hands off trying to flip the override when the engine's as hot as it is now. Even with a thermal suit…"

"Ardor can do it!"

"-Wait." The captain cut in. "You throw us into full speed with no ashfield and we'll splatter on the side of one of these shards. I don't fancy dying that way any better."

Fear gave Faldos clarity. "The nose drill." He said. "Charge it up, full spin. Should pierce us through larger shards and knock away some of the smaller ones."

"I don't—"

"I'm going. Do it or don't."

Faldos and Breff sprinted back down to the core. It blazed an angry orange, the cracking roots of the ship-tree struggling to contain its power.

They dashed to the puppet sitting halfway down the path. Faldos plugged his controller back in. Legless, he sent the puppet skittering along on its six arms, past the root network to the cylinder housing.

"See those three levers around the housing?" Breff asked. "Flip those!"

Using four of the arms to cling to the side, he used the puppets remaining two to flip the first couple switches. The third lever took a few tries, but he got it. Something fell away from one of Ardor's hands. He realized it was slag from a melted finger.

There was a screeching noise from the top of the hull, just above the core. It bent inward in an unnaturally wide ellipse.

Faldos forced his eyes downward. "What's next!?" he asked.

"Pull off the housing shell!"

Faldos had Ardor to pull against the shell. After some resistance, it jerked off and tumbled to the floor, nearly hitting them. This exposed the transparent vat of glowing gold material inside, encircled by cooling tubes and messy wires. A single metal lever was stuck vertically down the side of the vat, glowing red from proximity to the core.

"Pull that down!"

He tried, but the metal resisted Ardor's pulls. The lever moved, but then halted, as one of Ardor's hands came off, melting to slag.

The ellipse on the ceiling bent deeper, metal groaning under the strain.

Sweat was dripping off Faldos now and whether from heat or fear he didn't know or care. He released all safety restraints on Ardor's muscle fibers, grabbed the lever with three hands, braced the remaining two for leverage, and pulled.

The lever flipped. Ardor's hands melted. The puppet fell. The core dropped. The ceiling ripped open.

Thrust into the vat of pure fuel, the core exploded with blinding light. The tree's branches surged over the mess, before one final catalytic explosion sent Faldos and Breff flying backwards, tumbling through the hold, only for the ship's sudden acceleration to then drag them back in the other direction. They slammed against the far wall, just below the searing heat of the core. Distantly, beyond the pain, Faldos wondered how fast they'd have to be going for the inertial dampeners to struggle this much.

Then, like flicking off a light switch, the core went dead.

Darkness. The acceleration petered off. Soon they could stand again.

Emergency lights flickered on. Faldos and Breff stared first at the black, dead core, then to the massive gash in the ceiling above it. Shards of debris floated in the murk outside. If it hadn't been for the breathing field, they'd have been sucked out into vacuum the moment the metal had broken.

They shared the look of two men who should've been dead but were not. They climbed back up to the bridge. It was quiet. There were holes in the blast shield, where a handful of smaller shards had burst through like bullets. Half the operators were nursing wounds where they'd been struck. But miraculously, no one was dead.

Through the holes in the metal they could see out into the dark and dusty Shroud.

The captain stared out into that gloom. "...what was that?"

No one had an answer.

"Well...where are we, then?"

An operator answered, eyes stuck to his console. "A few hundred kilometers from where we started. Still way out from the nearest layover station. Core is completely dead. We've got a little forward momentum still but smaller impacts are gradually slowing that. And we're not exactly headed in the right direction anyway. Comms are working, but I doubt we can get a signal through all this kuron. Miracle we didn't smash into a shard big enough to rip us in half. And even still hull integrity is hanging by a thread. Breathing barrier is just barely holding up on backup power, it's gonna fail soon. We need to get out there and seal up some of these breaches before we lose all air."

"You heard him boys. Get out there."

Faldos no longer had the strength in him to complain. Already suited up, he and several other crewmen climbed out the hatch. Only from the outside did they get a good look at the final impact point, just above the core.

The hole was outlined by dozens of smaller punctures. Inside of some of these punctures were chunks of midnight black kuron. Faldos pulled out one such piece and found it unlike any of the other shards of the Obsidian Shroud.

It was almost as long as his forearm, sharp, curved and slightly serrated on the inside, smooth on the rest. He didn't need to check to know it'd be one-hundred percent pure kuron. Unmistakable was its shape, so unmarred by machine marks, so frightfully natural in its form.

A tooth.

# 1

# DEATHGAZE

---

A HUNTER'S GREATEST weapon is patience.

Lok had been young when a Slowstalker taught him the virtue of patience by giving him the scar along his back. He sure wasn't young anymore.

Some might even say that by his gruff voice and matted coat of fur, that he was getting old. But Lok didn't think of himself as old. Just experienced. Experience was a hunter's second greatest weapon. You got the second by exercising the first.

Today, patience was needed in the violet canyons of Gritharoug. Jagged crags spread out below Lok, a thin violet mist filling the snaking pathways. The mist drifted up from cave openings that peppered the canyon's walls and floor.

The Deathgaze could stalk out of any one of them.

Lok wouldn't get many shots. If this creature sensed danger it'd either flee deep below the surface for the rest of the season…or it would simply kill Lok. Neither end was acceptable.

Three piles of bait waited below. The mist had nearly swallowed the small one at the bottom. A second, slightly larger heap of gruel waited fifty meters higher up the slope. The third and largest pile was situated on a ledge Lok had carefully selected to be the perfect distance from himself.

The weapon he'd selected for this leg of the hunt was a Thryken 20k pulley bow.

Bows didn't tend to pack much stopping power but they were quiet, could be used unpowered, or charged with ash energy, and featured a selection of heads for the desired scenario. Hunting wasn't about firepower. It was about the right tool for the job.

Both he and his weapon had been coated in stealth spray, electronic imaging rendering him virtually invisible. He normally preferred a cloak, though. The spray was a real pain to rinse from his fur.

The hazy pinkish sun was dipping towards the horizon.

He'd been waiting for fifteen hours. He was prepared to wait another fifteen, if that's what it took.

Patience.

Lok could smell the Deathgaze before he could see it. Foul and sulfuric, the odor savaged his nostrils. That stench was the last warning some men ever got before death. Lok drew back the arrow feeling the rush of blood as his long-dormant muscles tensed.

The beast emerged.

A sinewy limb, with yellow rimmed black eyes dotting its length, reached out first. The limb ended in a claw that sheared into the rocky floor. Three more limbs followed carrying the barrel body of the beast out of the cave. There were eyes and eyes and eyes all the way down to its flicking tail that dripped with an acrid chemical.

The eyes roved, scanning every millimeter of the canyon. A pattern of long, hatched scales stood up across its body, ready to snap shut over the eyes at the first sign of danger.

But it wouldn't see this danger coming. One of the reasons Lok had picked a bow was that he could coat both the launcher and the projectile in stealthspray. Unlike a gun there'd be no muzzle flare or deafening noise giving him away. If he played this out right, he'd get three shots. Each one of them needed to count.

There was only one way to definitively kill a Deathgaze: destroy the nucleus. An armored organ working as both brain and heart. Even blowing up the monster was no guarantee of death, for as long as the nucleus remained, it could eventually regenerate. What's more, the location of the nucleus was different for each Deathgaze. Lok had no way of knowing where it would be on this one. That's what made this a multi-stage process.

The Deathgaze had seen the first pile of bait from the beginning, it'd been scanning for other predators or prey. Boldly secure in its own perception, the beast loped over to the first pile, and lapped it up in seconds. Just an appetizer. A hundred pupils locked on the second pile. It preferred live prey, but that'd been harder to find since the miners evacuated.

The Deathgaze pawed the ground in feigned disinterest. The charade didn't last.

It crawled up to the second pile, delving into this one too. Stomach a bit fuller, but not quite satisfactory. The third pile now had its attention. Twice as big as the second, the choice was clear.

As the Deathgaze climbed higher its wretched stink grew ever more potent. But Lok didn't move, didn't twitch. The stealthspray's effectiveness would plummet as soon as he started moving.

It stopped a few meters from the final pile, body tensing as it sensed something was off.

*Just take the bait,* he silently urged, *you've come this far.*

It took a half-step up, but hesitated. A pair of eyes on the back of its paw examined the food critically, while its hundreds of other eyes searched everything else. Many of them passed over Lok's position, making his skin crawl. Even with the stealthspray it felt wrong to be so out in the open. So exposed.

But then, both of them were exposed.

He needed to get behind the beast's front shoulder. He could see it, though the shot wasn't very clean. But after fifteen hours, it was tempting. If the Deathgaze ran…

The string suddenly felt very heavy.

Patience.

He waited. So did the Deathgaze.

It felt like an hour, the two of them standing there, frozen. From experience, Lok knew it'd only been a few minutes.

Ever so slowly the Deathgaze put its raised claw down and took another trepidatious step forward. Then another. And another.

It reached the final pile of bait. It lingered one final time. Lok felt like a compressed spring.

The beast leaned down and opened its mouth to eat.

Lok loosed the first arrow. In the fraction of a second before it struck, several of the eyes flickered, straining to see whatever glare they'd detected. Too late. The first arrow struck home, piercing the eye behind the Deathgaze's front shoulder.

The Deathgaze twisted around, trying to shut its chitin scales over the eyes. But he'd lanced through a nerve cluster that'd hamper such a movement. Instead, the scales only twitched without going flat. The beast spun, hiding the injury as its tail flicked, spraying a sizzling green glob from its tail in response to the sudden threat. But it had no notion where the arrow had come from, so it just sprayed the stone around it, sizzling as the liquid made contact.

Lok flicked his wrist, forearm quiver depositing another arrow into his grip. He pulled back in one clean motion before he loosed again, then jumped. Before he'd hit the ground, the second arrow struck, taking the Deathgaze through an eye on its side, piercing a primary mobility muscle.

He flicked his wrist, another arrow finding his hand.

The Deathgaze fired its tail again, this time whipping a glop at the perch Lok had vacated moments prior, burning into the stone. Its eyes flicked about and despite his stealth, quickly found him as he drew back.

Lok fired his third arrow at the same time as the Deathgaze. The arrow skimmed through the globby fluid and down the launcher gland of the Deathgaze's tail. The arrow would melt away in seconds, but that was fine. This final arrow had a glue tip designed to harden in reaction to the chemical from the Deathgaze's tail.

Lok ducked under the final glob. His bow was less fortunate, the oozing fluid striking and snapping the string.

But the bow had done its part. Deprived of both armor and chemical projectiles, the Deathgaze darted for the nearest hole big enough to accommodate it. That just so happened to be quite a distance from where it'd been feeding on the third pile. And the second arrow had slowed its dash, which still managed to be almost blindingly fast.

But Lok was fast too. About as fast as a wounded Deathgaze. He sprinted to intercept the beast, pulling his second weapon from his back. A blastspear.

His outline was visible now, the stealthspray neutered by his running. The Deathgaze instinctively flicked its tail at him, but the acid was still stopped up.

They'd reach the hole about the same time, which would leave it all down to chance.

Lok never left anything to chance.

The stealthsprayed trap snapped close on the Deathgaze's leg, jerking it out of its forward momentum.

He couldn't have put a trap down by the food, the Deathgaze's eyes were too keen, even stealthsprayed, they'd have noticed the subtle lighting differences from that close. But in the chaos of the chase...

The monster shrieked, swinging scythe claws at the metal trap. Once, twice, three times and the trap was mangled enough for the beast to tear it's leg free.

Didn't matter. Lok had arrived.

The beast swung claws as long as his forearm, with enough power to bisect him.

Lok had already been ducking before the swing. He deactivated the spray. He wanted the beast to see him clearly for this part.

He thrust the blastspear forward towards the beast's midsection.

In response there was a subtle tightening of muscles as the beast threw one claw to block the strike, while angling its hindquarters away. There. Near the hips, it'd reflexively put that part of its body out of harm.

Lok pulled back from the feigned strike and leaped over the Deathgaze. It lashed claws at him too slowly, it hadn't been ready for that move.

Lok landed on its back and plunged the blastspear down in front of the Deathgaze hips and beside its spine. He pulled the weapon's first trigger. A charge in the base of the haft blasted, sending the spearhead mounted on an inner rail lancing through the beast's innards. Passing easily though the flesh the blade struck something and halted abruptly before full extension. He'd hit the nucleus all right.

Lok pulled the second trigger. The battery pack on his back fueled a charge of deadly ash energy though the inner rail and to the head of the blastspear.

"You killed thirty-six men before I came here," Lok said to the beast. "No more."

The beast seized up, every eye on its body dilating before sharply contracting. It dropped stiffly to the ground, limbs stuck out rigidly. The nucleus was ash.

"....quarry slain."

Lok jumped down off the corpse. The fun part was over. Now for the gutting. Not that gutting couldn't be satisfying in its own right sometimes. But Deathgazes smell even worse on the inside.

Yet he couldn't skimp on this part. He'd already taken a pay cut by accepting the job. First he'd bleed the creature and while he waited, pluck all the eyes. They were valuable to collectors. Then he'd drain the tail of its acidic payload before getting to the meat. After a chase like that it'd be gamey at best, but Lok didn't waste meat, however it tasted.

Before all of that, a hunter's courtesy. He retrieved his cuffcomp from a sprayed-over pouch and locked it onto his wrist. He tapped on the device and made a call. It was answered after the first ring.

"The job's done," he said.

"Oh, thank you, sir, thank you! So, it should be safe to resume operations?"

"Yes."

"Why thank you again! Not just for killing the beast, but we had a betting pool and your survival has won me quite a bit of money."

"Hm," was his response. "Well, I'll be back at your office in an hour. I'd appreciate it if you had payment ready."

"Of course, of course."

He hung up. Moments later a second call came in.

"You know," Vosta said, "if you were gonna clean up this efficiently I would've pressed the foreman for more money."

Lok didn't bother questioning how Vosta had known so quickly about his successful hunt. She had a habit of knowing more than she really had any right to know.

"It ain't all about money," he said. "'Sides, I think we both know they didn't have much more to give."

"Your bleeding heart is as inspiring as ever, but you know we do have to pay the bills at some point. To that end, I'm going to need you to head out to our next job immediately."

"I still gotta skin and separate this corpse."

"No time."

"Do I happen to have some say in this?"

"Very well. I have three potential jobs for you. The choice is yours. All of them are somewhat time sensitive. However the third is especially so, and that's also the one you're going to pick.

"Mind telling me why I'm going to choose that one over the other two?"

"Of course. The first is a routine culling of Cresthorns the next system over. Pay is a thousand per head, so it could scale up quite a bit depending on how many you bring down. It's exclusive if we get there within the next few days. Next is a contract to exterminate a pair of Siltgorges that've been wreaking havoc on a Migdur mining operation. It's a solid one-point-three million contract, and that doubles if you can get it done in the next forty-eight hours. The final, is in the Scarlet System and concerns a monster of some kind that's been causing a few survey ship's to go missing. It's got a good payout, five million crowns…but it's not an exclusive contract. It's a bounty."

"Pass on the last one, then. Not worth competing with other hunters and them gettin' in the way."

"Oh, but that's the one you're going to pick."

"Right…and why am I doing that again?"

"There's a certain youth you asked me to keep an eye on by the name of Faldos."

"That kid? What's he done now? Don't tell me he owes somebody five million. Because if so, then he can get out of his own mess—"

"Faldos was on one of the survey ships that went missing."

Lok stared at the Deathgaze corpse without really looking at it. He worked his jaw over, subvocalizing curses.

"…How long ago?"

"Last contact was forty hours ago."

"Hm….he's probably dead, then."

"Could be," Vosta said simply. "You don't sound too shaken."

"He's just an old friend's kid. I barely know him…barely know him…"

Old words echoed in his mind.

*Lok, I need a favor. If something ever happens to me…"*

If a man had nothing else but his word, then he had enough.

Lok sighed. If the kid was dead…at the very least he had to hunt down the beast that did him in. He owed an old friend that much.

"Malvit," he finally cursed. "…All right, I'm on my way."

"Told you."

"You really know how to read a room."

"If you're the only one that can stand me, the sentiment is mutual."

"Fair 'nuff. Get me the details on the hunt and what happened to Faldos."

"I'll try but it seems they want to keep a lot of this under wraps until you're there in person."

"All right, I'm gone."

"Talk again soon."

He hung up. It seemed he'd have to take the corpse with him. He hoped the stench didn't linger too long on his ship.

"You were barely worth the ten-thousand they're paying me for this," He said to the corpse.

But for five million crowns, he'd be able to afford all kinds of cleaning services. He pulled out a length of cord and tied up the body for easier transport. Then he brought down a skimmer bike he'd stored inside a shallow cave above.

Lok hoisted the Deathgaze onto the bike, the vehicle barely supporting the weight without scraping the ground.

As he rode out of the canyon his eyes turned skyward, where a few stars were beginning to prick into existence along the horizon.

"You better not be dead, Faldos. Otherwise who's gonna knock sense into ya?"

A second thought immediately followed up that one.

"Now what kind of a beast they got out there that's worth five million crowns?"

He had a sinking suspicion that he already knew. And in truth it did scare him.

But fear was the first enemy that needed to be slain.

He was a hunter, after all.

# 2

# SCARLET MORN

SLICKMOLES HAVE MUDDY dens, Springhounds have mountain-top lairs, and Leviathans have cosmic roosts. Even the foulest of beasts have a place they call home. Lok's was a starship named *Hunt or Be Hunted II.*

He'd bought it well-used after the first *Hunt or be Hunted* was wrecked by a monster two weeks after he'd purchased it. Both the second ship and the nightmares had been with him ever since.

The *Hunt or Be Hunted II* was a shaft of metal, with a satellite ring encircling the main body by means of metal cables. The ring sported the bulk of the craft's weaponry. It featured a couple of modern illsur blades on mechanical arms, but mainly carried such old-fashion weapons as missile launchers, rotary guns, coilguns, and a particle beam.

The bow of the ship ended abruptly into an open hole, forming the barrel of the largest weapon on the ship. Just an antique he'd paid a great deal of money for. Further back, attached to the lower part of the main body were twelve launch tubes for the ship's array of H11 rockets. Near the stern, the shaft spread out where the ship's main thruster was. The whole thing was scored, dented and charred. The trophies of a dangerous, but persistent lifetime of activity.

But one thing the ship lacked was a bone drive enabling warp travel. To that end, the *Hunt or be Hunted II* was currently fixed to the massively skeletal cylinder of a star freighter. His ship sat along with thirty-odd other ships like his, all for the purpose of being ferried between star systems. The fee had cost almost half his earnings for the Deathgaze hunt. It was an annoying reality of his job, but it beat paying a fortune and tying his soul to the bone peddlers to get a bone drive of his own.

True black surrounded the freighter. It was not the dark of a moonless cloudy night. It was not even the dark of a deep cave belly without a lamp. It was as if light and existence itself was only on the congregation of ships and beyond there was nothing, and never had been. The strange environment of a warp sphere. Like most sane creatures, Lok found warping both fascinating and terrifying.

A speckling of lights appeared in front of the freighter, a symptom of entering real space. They abruptly snapped back to reality, a bed of stars now taking over their surroundings.

The star of Scarlet System shone over the port side of the ship. Filters in the breathing barrier protected his eyes from the raw light. He still had to squint to see a small, almost imperceptible rock in the star's path which would be its only significant planet: Scarlet Morn.

It was of a much darker shade of red, that of old blood. The planet was ringed by a swirling cloud of black dust and rubble that stretched out for what must have been at least a hundred thousand kilometers.

That would be the wilds his quarry was among. A forest, or perhaps, a sea, among the stars. The thought of it brought him chilly anticipation.

Lok left the top deck, by way of a hatch that dropped him into the modest bridge of the Hunt or Be Hunted II. It was only slightly more spacious than the cockpit of a transport shuttle. Just a few instruments, a few lockers for equipment, the helm, and a viewport at the front. A true viewport, not a projector screen. Just the way he liked it.

He took hold of the familiar comfort of the helm and guided a course towards the planet. It'd be a hair over three hours. He flipped a switch, locking in the path before sitting back in a chair he'd probably slept in more than his actual bed. He'd just rest his eyes for a bit.

Lok didn't know it then, but that was the last good rest he'd get for quite some time.

• • •

LOK AWOKE TO the sound of his cuffcomp ringing. He usually left the blasted thing on silent, but Vosta would skin him alive if he didn't leave it on when there was a new job to be had. He checked his cuff. Speaking of…

"You got a reason you're interrupting my nap?" He said, answering the call.

"You got a reason you're sleeping the day away, when there's a hunting job we need to get the jump on?" Vosta said. "You're about to miss docking."

Lok checked his cuff again, for the time. Then he cursed.

"Huh. Thought I set an alarm."

"It's that old model you've got hooked up to your wrist. You really ought to upgrade."

"I have a thing about antiques."

"You are an antique."

"What's that make you?"

"Mature."

"That's a double-standard if I've ever heard one."

He eased himself up from the chair and stretched, feeling every joint pop. He shook off whatever aches he could before focusing his eyes out the viewport.

He was greeted by the ring-shaped orbital platform of Ruby Roost. True to its name, it was cast in red light by the system's star. But the bulk of the view was dominated by the planet just below. Scarlet Morn, a dark maroon planet, jagged and pockmarked by meteor impacts.

"Are you standing around, admiring the view again?"

"Sorry, mother."

"As if! Any son of mine would have better manners."

"Well, you know us hunters. All raised by Spinghounds."

"That's your excuse?"

"And I'm sticking with it. Why's it red? Do I need to get my eyes checked?"

"Ah, that. Yes, stars are typically white in space. But out here the Shroud acts as a filter. Even outside the main shard field, the quintillions of rock and metal particulates have blanketed the system. They filter the light, and from here, leave the welcoming blood red tint you see now."

"Nice place for a holiday home."

"Oh, certainly."

Lok took the helm. The main thruster had automatically dropped off earlier, and drag thrust had been introduced once they'd entered range of the station. He kicked on the cruising thruster and guided himself along the station's wheel, until he reached a large rectangle cut into the hull. Inside waited a hanger bay, full of ships like his. He pulled to a stop, transmitted his credentials and waited for port authority to signal his entry. They sent a go-ahead code a few minutes later, and he pushed on inside.

Magnetizers guided his ship into a suspended berth, a metal framework that snatched up the *Hunt or be Hunted II*. A walkway extended out and locked onto the deck of his ship. The hangar was all shiny metal and fresh paint jobs. There weren't enough scratches from missed berthing or burn scars from errant thrusters. It was all too fresh. This station was younger than his ship's oil filter.

"Took you long enough," Vosta said over his cuff.

"You ain't even here, whatchu complaining about?"

"Just eager to collect my finder's fee."

"Leech fee, you mean."

"Please, you'd still be bagging Slickmoles on Durathos Four if you didn't have me chasing down the big jobs. Now hop to it, you've got a very large station to get across. I've sent a map to that antique you like so much."

Lok checked his cuffcomp for a map of the station. It only took a couple taps before the screen woke up. Still perfectly functional. A circular map appeared with a line drawn from his current position, to his destination.

He strapped on the minimum number of tools and weapons he thought station security would allow, before covering it all with his favorite cloak. It could use active camouflage, like stealth spray. Instead he tuned the cloak to be totally non-reflective, rendering it an ultra-black, to imitate his natural fur.

He strode off the *Hunt or Be Hunted II* and onto the network of walkways snaking through the hangar bay. The place even smelled new.

He brushed shoulders with spacers and station engineers, running back and forth across the too-narrow pathways. From the jump Lok knew the place was off. Everyone's eyes seemed intent on being pointed anywhere but out into space, and the Obsidian Shroud waiting there. Beyond that, there was the smell, the one behind the scent of newness.

Fear.

Eventually the hangar bay gave way to sterile corridors, painted white. His true black fur stood out here. More than once people jumped at his silhouetted appearance before they recognized him as a mere unusual breed of Logra. People were definitely on edge here.

The path split many times and more than once his cuffcomp struggled to figure out his orientation. But at long last he navigated his way to the rail station. A few others waited, but no one of concern. No threats.

A train of railcars pulled in and opened beckoning doors. Lok stepped inside and, moments later, the doors closed and he was swept away down the line.

Both the cars and rail line were windowed to offer a view outside the station. The line was oriented towards the inside of the ring, displaying both the red planet below, and the refining facilities built along the center of the station that dumped impurities onto it.

"Ruby Roost is basically one big kuron mill," Vosta said over his cuffcomp. "Everything else is in service of that production."

"Surprised they bothered building one this far out in the sticks."

"They go where the kuron is. Listen up, 'cause this part's important: That planet down there, Scarlet Morn, used to have two moons. Now it has none. The two went and crashed into each other, shattering into countless pieces."

"Must've been Sundering for anyone on the planet."

"Would've been if anyone lived there. The planet's barren, not even worth terraforming. Less than a thousand people were even in the entire system. But since those moons crashed together, the population has skyrocketed."

"I'm guessing that has something to do with this shiny new mill station?"

"Sure does. See, turns out both of them moons were packed with kuron and now it's all out and in the open, ripe for the picking. Of course, it's scattered across three-light minutes of space and mixed with plenty of less valuable silica, iron and other elements. It's enough to build a whole industry. They'll be mining this place for decades."

Lok watched shiploads of kuron ore being dumped into refinery points. The ore's eventual future as ingots of pure kuron was visible as they were shipped out from the upper half of the station's ring.

"Lotta wealth down there." He said. "They say this stuff is, what? Twice as valuable as gold?"

"Four times, at the current rate. Not many materials that can take a beating like kuron. Even the low purity kuron-tungsten alloy on most starships is more durable than twice as much tungsten without."

"Ash me. Whoever owns this station is set for life. For the next dozen generations, really."

"That would be our employer, The Burgrave Rottus. He owns Ruby Roost, which happens to contain the system's biggest mill, but not it's only. Plenty of guilds and corps setting up shop to get a piece of the pie. By all accounts business is booming."

"But?"

"But a few ships have gone missing. You're almost there, so I'll let them explain the rest."

The railcar pulled to a stop, and Lok strode out, consulting his cuff again.

"Mr. Lok?"

He looked up to find a Meldar with twitchy wings walking up.

Lok grunted. "Might be. Who's asking?"

"I'm Kelith, assistant manager of this station." He wore a suit that looked moderately expensive and a thin lipped smile.

"Ah, right. Well…nice to meet ya."

"Forgive my associate," Vosta said from his cuff. "By his own admission he was raised by springhounds. Makes him terrible for social events but he's an ashing good hunter."

"I'm all right," Lok said.

"He's modest, too."

"That's excellent to hear," Kelith broke in. "If you'll follow me, the Burgrave awaits."

Kelith took him down a few similarly white corridors, before they passed through a door into a hall quite unlike the previous ones. It was carpeted, painted scarlet, and even featured a few paintings. Most were portraits of Meldar men and women in noble uniforms. The final painting was a stylized portrait of Scarlet System. The hall terminated in a door that opened as they approached.

The chamber within was pure red. Red walls, red ceiling, red carpeted. The room was a half-circle, with six pillars along the curve of the wall. The pillars looked to be made of kuron, and had been carved to appear old, but were obviously new additions. In between the pillars were windows displaying a view of Scarlet Morn framed by stars.

At the center of it all, was a chair on a raised platform. A weak imitation of a throne.

A Meldar man sat in the chair. His small wings jutted out from the back of a frilly expensive suit. Even through the fabric the lankiness of his arms and legs were obvious. His crown, the circular metal growth sprouting from around his skull, was large. He was nobility for sure. Red stripes painted a face that tried to be stoic, but ended up in more of a grimace.

Lok could smell the cold sweat on him from here.

Two other men were in the room, both standing at the bottom of the platform.

One was an Akadorn with a scarred beak and one smoky blind eye. He was draped in a well-worn but sturdy space suit and had a scratched up hookreel slung over his shoulder. Blades sprouted from his wings in place of feathers. Obviously, another hunter and an experienced one by the look of it. But the other occupant, Lok, didn't need to guess about. He hadn't even needed to see the other man. His stench alone would've given him away.

Sendro Kaul had an absurdly large axe slung over his shoulder. His fur was a bright red with ripples of glowing orange and yellow stripes hatching over each other. Such garish bioluminescent colors were actually quite beneficial for camouflage in the neon jungles of his homeworld.

Those ripples of color were in sharp contrast to Lok's own fur, pitch black, reflecting no light at all. Another difference was the bushy tail flickering behind the younger Logra.

Lok felt the phantom pain where his own tail used to be.

Sendro's eyes narrowed as Lok entered, his lips parted in a sharp, toothed grin.

"If it ain't old Lok Brightslayer. Don't you have a gravestone to be picking out?"

"Sendro, I…wish you were somewhere else. Like on the surface of the nearest star."

"That the best comeback you got, old man?"

"When you get to my age you have less patience for stupidity."

"Gentlemen," said the Meldar in the chair. "Let's try and keep things civil. We haven't even discussed the reason you're all here, yet."

"Oh, you'll know when we stop being civil," Sendro said. "But I'll admit we should get down to business."

"Very well." The Meldar cleared his throat. "I am Halfur Rottus, Burgrave of Scarlet System and Lord Commander of this station. My family built The Roost five generations ago when Scarlet System was given to us by the Archduke. It has been worthless almost the entire time we've owned it. That was until a little over a year ago when Scarlet Morn's two moons collided, scattering into a debris field of precious kuron. We call it the Obsidian Shroud."

Sendro let out an exaggerated yawn. "What does this have to do with hunting?"

If he were standing just a little closer, Lok would've reached over and smacked the kid across the head. "Watch yourself, Sendro. You're talking to nobility in his own house."

Halfur's eye twitched. "It's…all right. I have a habit of drawing things out." He sighed and his wings dropped, some of the forced strength leaving him. "Look, I'll just get down to it: We contract survey ships to locate high purity kuron deposits. Over the past three months we've completely lost contact with fifteen survey ships."

"How many do you usually employ?"

"Over two-hundred. And that's just the companies with a contract to my station. Third parties have more. Now, a few ships disappearing in of itself was not strange. You get a few of those. There's so much kuron and other metal dust that communications inside the cloud are virtually nonexistent. Too much interference. So, there's no tracking them until they come back to port. But…they did miss their usual return check-ins. When the first few went missing, we figured they decided to quit without leaving word. After ten vanished we started to suspect one of our competitors was scooping them up. But the eleventh…well, we found pieces of it."

"Pieces?"

"Another survey crew took over their territory and found what was left of their ship. A tungsten-kuron alloy hull shredded like it was copper foil. Not a crewman in sight, although there was enough… biological matter to conclude their deaths hadn't been pleasant."

Halfur tapped his wrist, and a holographic projection appeared In front of them: a jagged lump of metal that no longer looked anything like a ship.

"We soon found others, after retracing their paths." More images of starship wrecks, nearly as damaged, but occasionally with a bit of hull or a satellite ring intact.

"All of them had two similarities: no survivors, and the ship's core was always gone. Not just damaged, but gone, ripped out by…something. We thought…no, hoped, it was pirates."

"And how long did it take you to warn the surveyors?" Lok asked.

Halfur cleared his throat. "We…advised extra caution but didn't want to cause unnecessary panic before we knew what we were dealing with."

"Sounds like you were sweeping it under a rug."

Halfur frowned. "I disagree with that assessment."

Sendro snickered. "Now who's talking back to nobles?"

"You were being a pain for its own sake." Lok said. "But me? I got a thing about unnecessarily endangering lives."

Halfur shifted his stance, eyes preoccupied with the floor. "The situation was complex. Surveyors often leave for weeks at a time, and we can't exactly signal them to come back in."

"You could have sent ships after them, to warn them."

"In retrospect…that would have been a good idea."

"And now? Have you warned them about this yet? Not just to your own men but the other companies?"

"After our fourteenth loss we started…tentative communications about the issue. They weren't exactly forthcoming out the gate. But we now believe the number of lost ships may be as high as thirty. It'll be hard to say for sure, since many surveyors are still out there. The other guilds didn't seem to know much more than we did. It was still a mystery. Until a fifteenth one vanished. We assumed it'd have the same fate as the previous but…three days ago we got a transmission. There was a lot of interference but we've managed to clean some of it up."

Another tap on Halfur's cuff and an audio recording played.

"Kzzrt…this is the Scavenging Savant, we were attacked by some kind of creature that—kzzzrt—had teeth made of kuron and—kzzzzrt—and not sure if we can get the backup run—kzzzzzrt—our current coordinates are one-hundred six, thirty-four, Fifty—kzzzzzzzzzzrt—send help as soon as possible, before—"

The recording ended.

Lok felt the fur on his back stand up. It was all too familiar. His hand instinctively reached for one of the many blades on his person. Not that such a small weapon would protect him from the creature that did this.

Vosta sent Lok a private message.

*Faldos was aboard that one.*

Honestly, Lok didn't think that recording really improved the odds of the boy or the rest of the crew's survival. Not after what he'd just seen.

A part of him, a small but not small enough part, told him to pack up his ship and travel back in the direction he'd come from. Whether the kid was still alive or not, he probably wouldn't be so for long.

Lok throttled that primal fear. He didn't flee from beasts. They fled from him.

Halfur cleared his throat. It seemed like a tell of his. "We haven't received another communication since, and none of our pre-programmed scouting probes have returned. If the message is still accurate they'll be somewhere in the one-hundred six, thirty-four, fifty area. Fifty-what, we're not sure. We couldn't get the complete last coordinate. Leaves a few thousand kilometers of potential search area. We have since sent other probes instructing all survey teams to return, but it could be some time before all of them are found, if the probes make it through at all."

"And let me guess," Sendro said, chuckling. "Everyone else is too scared to go out there in person to see if anyone's still alive or let us know what we're after?"

"It's been difficult to organize a search party. But our belief is that if one of you are able to reach them, they might be able to illuminate what kind of creature—"

"I already know what it is," Lok said.

Halfur blinked. "You do?"

"I could've told you straight off, the damage on those starships wasn't done by no pirates. They were ripped 'part by something … hungrier. The list of void-breathin' creatures that could have done this is a short one. The bit about the missing cores makes it even shorter, only a few beasts respond to that flavor of snack. But kuron teeth? Factor in the rest and you got just about one likely culprit: a Nulljaw. I'd know, one ate my last ship."

Halfur swallowed, his lip twitching, and wings shifting. The Akadorn hunter remained passive.

Sendro laughed. "Nulljaw, eh? Never killed one of them before. Heard it's fun, though. If ya survive."

Lok could still see teeth as black as night bursting through the hull of the *Hunt or be Hunted I*.

"...Fun isn't the word I'd use."

"If you're a little nervous, you could sit this one out, old-timer. No shame in admitting you haven't got it anymore."

"But then who'll kill it when you ash this up?"

"Only thing that's getting ashed is that Nulljaw! That five-million is mine!"

"It'll go to the victor," The Akadorn hunter said, more to himself than the others.

Lok felt a headache coming on. Hunting was about preparation and control. Two more wildcards in the mix would make that difficult. Nearly impossible when one of those wild cards was an idiot like Sendro.

"Right, so," the idiot said. "Nulljaw's out there. Stranded ship too. Five million to kill the beast. Anything else we should know?"

"I think that's the general overview—"

Sendro gave a mock bow then went out of his way to walk around the Akadorn so he could bump into Lok as he strode out of the room. His back was exposed as he left, it'd be so easy to toss a knife at it…

Sendro was fortunate that Lok was such a nice guy.

"He's an…excitable one," the Akadorn hunter said.

Lok snorted. "That's putting it mildly. I'm Lok, by the way."

"I'm K'val. A pleasure." He bowed his head and gave his feathered arm a flourish. "But I'm afraid I must agree with the young Logra in one respect: prudence is of the essence here. May the best lure dredge up the prey…"

"And may the victorious hunter enjoy his feast at the end," Lok finished.

"So good to find someone else versed in the Rules of the Hunt. When this is all over, I wouldn't mind trading tales over a bottle of grog."

"If we live, why not? Winner buys."

"That'll be a small consolation."

"Guess I better win, then."

"That'll be me, I'm afraid," K'val said, bowing to Halfur. "Thank you, Lord Halfur, the beast should be bagged within a few days." He left.

Lok moved to exit too, but stopped at the threshold. "Respectfully, Lord Halfur, Burgrave of Scarlet System…you should've made this an exclusive contract. Bounties are well and good for culling populations and tracking down an elusive beast. But this would have worked better with one crew working to hem in the monster."

"Would you feel the same if you hadn't been the one we'd offered the contract to?"

"Yeah. Because then I wouldn't be stuck out there with Sendro."

"No one's keeping you here if you find these terms unacceptable."

"Nah. Like I said before. Someone's gotta make sure the Nulljaw gets slayed after Sendro ashes things up. Just have the five million ready. No matter how this goes down, my ship's gonna need repairs."

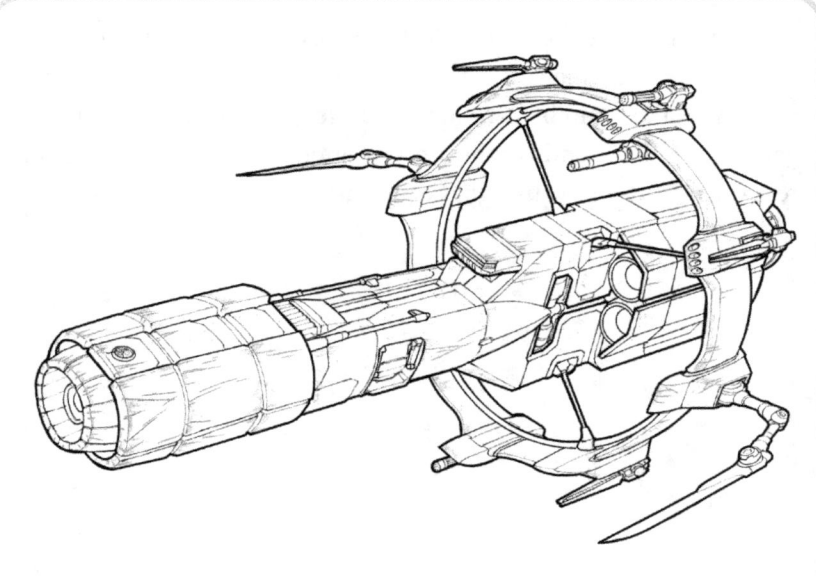

# THE HUNT OR BE HUNTED II

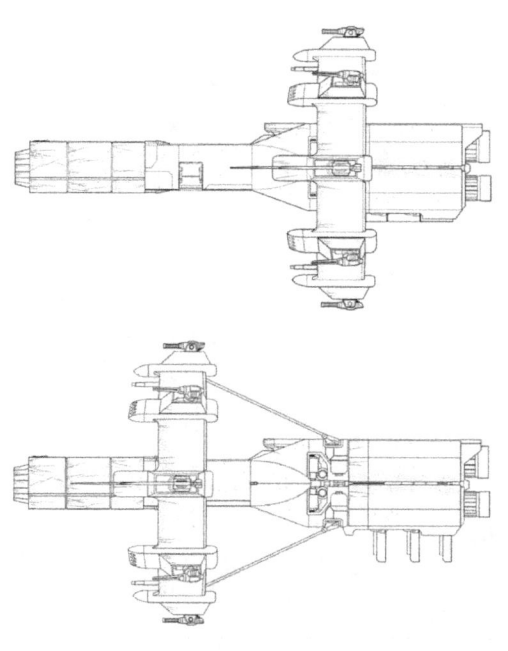

# 3

# INTO THE SHROUD

---

BY CHANCE, THE *Hunt or be Hunted II* was moored just a few ships over from Sendro's ship, the *Chopping Block*, according to the oversized letters painted onto its flank. It was a newer model, some bulky rig with not one, but two satellite rings. Both were absolutely bristling with modern illsur weapons. Ship grade swords, axes, drills, saws, ballistae, and gripping claws. The flaunting of a wealthy hunter.

Sendro marched across the deck, trying to look important while his subcontractors, all other Logra, did most of the heavy lifting. Mostly winding up or loosening rigging for the satellite rings, replacing worn blades with fresh ones and filling the ballistae with quarrels. Of course, Sendro would notice Lok glancing at the other ship.

"See how you get to kick back a little when you actually give your subordinates a decent paycheck!?" Sendro called over.

Lok scoffed. "I paid you a lot more than you were worth!"

"Then why am I flying this beauty while you're still in that bucket of bolts?"

"Because my bucket of bolts is gonna get the job done."

"We'll see, old man."

"Quit it with the old man nonsense! I'm not even in my sixth decade!"

"Sounds past your prime to me!"

"Past my prime is still better than you on your best day."

"You ain't seen me on my best day."

"And now you know why I paid you what I did."

Sendro didn't have a witty reply to that one. Lok took the win and turned away to make sure his own ship was in working order. The guns and rocket launchers were already full up, he always kept them stocked. He did oil some of the winches on the satellite ring's rigging. They weren't particularly prone to sticking, but he didn't want them to start now.

He gathered a few other items he'd need.

The first was his biggest and strongest angling reelrod. The pole was twice as tall as Lok and nearly as thick as his arm at the base. It could be used as a crane to haul cargo if he wanted it to. It featured a bundle of hooks that were about the size of his fist but could expand into a bramble of barbs a meter in diameter. But would it be strong enough to reel in his prey?

The second group of items were microcores. Twelve of them. They were spheres, each sitting about as high as Lok's waist and almost heavier than they were worth. Normally they would provide backup power for a starship. Today, they would be bait.

Finally, he had a Splint and Chaff Arms Twinshot double barrel electro-thermal light-gas gun, along with a set of replacement barrels. The 24 mm barrel weapon fired pure kuron slugs so fast it destroyed a barrel each time it was fired. He might only get two shots at a time, but few things ever survived the first. Ammo was a fortune, but worth the cost. There were far stronger guns attached to his ship, but in terms of handhelds, it had no equal. He slung it across his back, where he could reach it at a moment's notice.

There'd be no taking of chances this time.

• • •

THE OBSIDIAN SHROUD was crescent shaped, curled in orbit around the planet of Scarlet Morn, like a Nightshell's claw closing around an unsuspecting fish.

The debris cloud's width varied. It was long and stretched on the sides, mostly fine dust with a gradual incline in the size of shards as one approached the center. However, near the facility of Ruby Roost, where Lok had departed, the gradient was much sharper and the distance to the center of the cloud was relatively short, only about a half-light minute.

It was into this wall of darkness that his ship was fast approaching. Behind, the maroon of Scarlet Morn and the shiny space station above it. To his left, the system's red star was already starting to get overshadowed by one of the debris cloud's crescent arms.

"Remember your ship's ashfield might burn up the smaller pieces of kuron, but don't take any chances with those larger pieces. They could rip her apart if you let them," Vosta said over his cuff.

"I've been in debris clouds before."

"Not like this one. The density in there is insane. We'll lose comms minutes into you entering the outer layer."

"Imagine my disappointment."

"Hilarious. But don't worry, you should have company before long."

"I'm sure me and the Nulljaw will get along like old drinking pals."

"Lok…" There was a spike of concern in her voice.

"Yes?"

"Are you sure you can take this thing?"

"Don't insult me."

"I'm not. I just…well, it didn't go so well last time you met one."

"I was younger then. Didn't know half of what I know now."

"True…but I imagine you were more spry back then too."

"Whatever I've lost in physique I've more than made up for by collecting the biggest, nastiest weapons ever made for the purpose of hunting. And a whole lot of experience using 'em. If you don't hear back from me in a week… It's because the beast is really good at hiding. Shouldn't be more than two."

"That's what I like to hear." Her voice was already getting staticky. "Should I have them get something ready for you when you get back?"

"Yeah. Nulljaws are terrible eatin'. See if they've got any Nukgresk steaks on that base there."

"I'll see what I can do." Her voice was deeply warbled, it wouldn't be long now. The shroud was swallowing him.

His ship cruised on, the star becoming a dull glow behind the dust. The view of the planet behind got equally dim. Soon there was more light coming from the flickering motes of his ship's ashfield burning up shards.

He was on a course set to the damaged ship's last location. He didn't really expect to find survivors, but where there was a chance he'd try. If possible, though, he'd end this before he even reached the derelict.

Vosta's static voice warbled out one last message: "Good hunting, Lok."

And so it began.

• • •

THE UNFORTUNATE TRUTH of hunting is that it is astonishingly easy to go from predator to prey. Lok's failure to heed that lesson had cost him his first ship.

His hand gripped the *Hunt or be Hunted II*'s helm with greater strength than was strictly necessary. He didn't know if the Nulljaw knew he was in the Shroud, but he'd act as though it did.

Three hours in the Shroud he'd reached the Scavenging Savant's estimated position. He'd found nothing yet.

But the search area itself was wide. And with the shifting of the shard field and any momentum the ship had had before, they could be hundreds if not thousands of kilometers away by now…if there was anything left.

Motes of light flashed across the front of the ship as more and more shards were caught in the ashfield. It was distracting to say the least, and was probably hurting his chances at spotting the wreck. Remote controlled probes wouldn't work very far due to interference.

Lok swapped between the standard radio channels but heard nothing but static. Maybe he could boost his range by running a chain of probes out, each one just within range of the last one down the line. He dismissed the idea. It wouldn't buy him much range and he'd have to slow the ship to keep the probes from falling behind. What's more, he'd only be able to broadcast in one general area at a time.

But he was getting nowhere fast. And while he did still have a rough estimate of his location in the Shroud, the longer he was out here the worse his frame of reference would become.

And then, of course, there was the Nulljaw. It'd only benefit from Lok getting lost in this midnight dust.

He needed to start thinking outside the box.

An idea like a spark set aflame in his mind. A way to search for both the wrecked ship and the Nulljaw while at once.

He did have to slow his ship down with a reverse thrust, but it would be worth the trade. In response to his slowed speed fewer shards triggered the ashfield.

Pulling up the weapons console he accessed his complement of long-range H11 rockets. H11s were multi-purpose and recon was already one intended use.

He instructed the rockets to broadcast a simple message inquiring for any ship in need of aid, break for a response, then transmit again. And also to record visuals for everything they passed. The rockets already had all the equipment necessary for this, H11s were versatile like that.

He had them follow some basic evasion protocols which should let them dodge larger chunks of debris that they might otherwise collide with. Their installed ashfields would deal with the smaller bits. Once the rockets completed a preset path regularly transmitting his message, they'd return to his ship's vector and he'd see if they'd found anything. He had twelve long range rockets. He'd hold onto two but ten would still let him cast a pretty large net. He finished up the coding and launched them.

A camera feed showed the rockets drop from their launch tubes on the bottom of the ship. Out the viewport he watched them tear off into the dark, leaving tails of bright orange plasma behind. That done, it was time to go fishing.

• • •

LOK HOOKED UP his best angling chair onto the *Hunt or be Hunted II*'s satellite ring and settled in for a long wait.

Nothing was visible but black dust and rock as far as the eye could see. It was like the *Hunt or be Hunted II* had plunged down into the deepest ocean, or fallen beneath the vapors of a gas giant.

He didn't bother with a searchlamp, that'd only provide an illusion of perception. He wouldn't see anything until it was too late.

Yes, he was vulnerable, out on the satellite ring, the very edge of what could be considered part of his ship. But that nearness went both ways. He was closer to his prey too.

On the rail to the left of the chair was a baiting catapult. On the right was his angling reelrod, spooled with the thickest wire he had. The end of the line was hooked with one of the microcores. Lok fired the core up, glowing orange. He loaded it into a catapult and let it fly.

The core tore off into the gloom, reelrod's spool spinning out wire as it went. The glow of the core quickly faded into the black, the cable pivoting as the core fell behind the ship's forward momentum. He let the reel go on and on, until it was about five-hundred meters out, and only then did he tap the break, stopping the reelrod's spool in place. There was some trembling along the wire as the core bumped along shards of debris. He couldn't quite see the pale glow anymore, but that was good.

Finally, using his cuffcomp, he instructed his ship's engine to cool down, and further slow their forward thrust. He took a deep breath, unhindered by a space suit as he'd set the ship's breathing barrier past the ring.

Just darkness, even the stars winking out of existence. It was a harrowing place to be. And yet… there was something calming about the infinite quiet of the void, only the dim hum of his ship down below.

Lok cracked open a drink and sat back to wait. Patience was his greatest weapon, after all.

Three hours and three empty cans later came the crick, crick, crick of the reelrod spool spitting out more cable as something tugged on the other end.

# 4

# ON THE HOOK

---

LOK EYED THE reelrod spool, daring more line to pull. It didn't disappoint.

Crick crick crick crick.

Lok sat up, muscles tensing. This wasn't the bait being jostled by debris. Use a reelrod long enough and you learn to tell when the thing pulling on the other end is alive.

Crick crick crick crick crick.

Lok slid his chair's frame behind the reelrod, taking hold with both hands. The rod's hydraulics locked into the satellite ring would do the real heavy lifting, but fine control was just as important here. He fingered the spool's break, but didn't pull. Yet.

Crick crick crick crick crick crick crick crick crick crick crick crick crick crick crick crick crick-

The cricking devolved into a high-pitched whine as the spool turned on and on, becoming a blur.

He tapped the spool's break, just to slow the turning. Barely. He pressed it harder. The spool resisted, the rod itself bending.

This was a strong one. An adult, probably. And if it could rip apart a ship's hull, it wouldn't have much trouble with a single cable, even an illsur one. But that was where fine control came in. Lok instructed his ship to kill the forward thrust. He'd already shut off the ship's primary core so it was just aux thrusters now.

The spinning stopped without Lok's application of the break. The thing on the other end was repositioning. He tapped the retractor, bringing in a couple meters of cable before the line resisted again. He instructed the ship's thrusters to creep towards the direction of the cable. As the ship moved he retracted more line before it again slowed and stopped.

The quarry sensed something was off, but hadn't figured out what yet.

Lok kept tapping the ship's thruster, pushing them closer to the end of the line. He didn't need to pull the thing to his ship. He could pull his ship to it.

A shard of rock the size of a freezer came within meters of Lok's skull before it burned up in the ship's ashfield. But he couldn't lose his nerve now.

Back and forth the reelrod's spool went, retracting then pulling back out. Lok allowed the small losses, applying too much of the breaks would snap the line. All that mattered was a gradual decrease in distance, which he was getting.

Closer he crawled towards his prey, slowly gaining the upper hand in their fight across the reelrod's spool.

Through the gloom he started to see the vague outline of… something, writhing back and forth, sending ripples through the dust. It was still about three-hundred meters out. Adrenaline poured into Lok's veins. He pushed the ship on, reeling in the cable as he went, closer, closer, closer.

The beast's outline froze and turned, the silhouette narrowing. It was facing him now, probably studying his own outline in the gloom.

They waited, the two of them, neither certain of who should move first. Lok's hand drifted to his cuffcomp and the screen of weapons systems waiting there. He was itching to fire his entire ship's arsenal at this beast. Or to at least draw the Twinshot at his side. He forced his hand back. Not yet. Not until it was closer.

A dim glow, muffled by the dust, shone out from inside the beast. That would be the mini-core attached to the line. What was it...?

The light vanished and in the same instant the shadow jerked to the side. The reel spat out cable. Lok reflexively slammed the break. Something twisted in the shadows. The line went slack. It'd been snapped.

The shadow turned and another, much brighter glow shone from one end. Debris scattered away as it retreated deeper into the gloom. Lok's instinct was to give pursuit, but no. By the time his engine warmed back up, it'd be long gone. The glow was already fading.

He considered firing a missile after it, just out of spite. But it wouldn't be a kill shot. He saved his ammo.

Had he spooked it? The ship's core had been off so maybe it simply hadn't identified him as food. Or...it hadn't wanted to fight on Lok's terms.

Clever one.

Lok suspected that even if he dropped another microcore it wouldn't bite. He'd try again when it got hungry. Until then...more waiting.

· · ·

THREE HOURS AFTER he'd launched them, the rockets started to return, one by one. None had recorded any radio replies. Lok programmed new routes and sent them on their way again.

He retreated from his seat on the satellite ring to watch the rocket's recordings while he waited for the end of the second route. Holograms projected around the viewport showed the first round of camera feed all at once, running at three times speed. That proved about as interesting as watching a Gresk molt. Nothing but black dust and rock. He'd hoped they might've spotted the ship and simply hadn't received a reply, but thus far that hadn't proved to be the case.

As he watched, Lok cracked open a ration pack and feasted on the bland pseudo-meat inside. He considered trying to fry up some of that Deathgaze corpse in his freezer. But, while Lok was a decent cook, he probably lacked the expertise to properly prepare Deathgaze meat without poisoning himself. And so there he sat, stewing in the quiet, nothing but the distant hum of the ship's core.

But Lok had finally grown tired of the void's simple quiet. So, shoving the last of his rations down his gullet, he rose and retrieved from a nearby locker one of his few companions for a solo hunt like this: a shadowstring.

Pulling it out of its case, he checked over the familiar instrument.

Made from the bones, hide and sinew of a Shadelick from his homeworld, the instrument's body was as dark as Lok's was. Only the strings were coated in a glowing oil, in contradiction of its name. He plucked at the instrument, finding it out of tune as usual. He tweaked the knobs and adjusted by ear until he was satisfied.

He strummed idly while watching the rockets' videos but before long his fingers found a familiar tune.

*"Some say huntin's best with a pack,*
*More eyes, and noses to help ya track,*
*A few folks 'round to guard yer rear,*
*Won't lay your head alone with fear.*

*But often they'll be the folks you fight,*
*No peace, just bickering in the night,*
*Always eating your food and your patience tryin',*
*Or else end up caught in a trap and dyin',*

*Don't gotta share your food and coin with a crowd,*
*No troubles, no stress, nothing you share, nothing loud,*
*Alone, nobody, no bothers is how I like it,*
*Just as long as you don't mind the quiet."*

A few songs later and Lok's rockets had again returned with their latest findings. His lips curled into a sharp-toothed grin.

Two rockets, numbers eight and nine, had recorded responses. He played back eight's first and immediately wished he hadn't.

"...O' great hunter of beasts, Lok Brightslayer, please save us wee helpless folk from the scary beasties outside! If ya don't keel over from old age first!"

Lok was gonna throttle Sendro the next time he got within arm's reach of him. He marked the estimated location of the idiot's ship on his map. Not all that far, actually. He switched over to the next recording.

"Regretfully, I haven't seen anything. But good hunting to you." At least K'val had been an adult about it. Lok's rocket idea was seeming less genius by the minute. But it was still the best idea he had, so he plotted some new routes.

Before he had a chance to fire the rockets, something caught his eye from the first round of rocket recordings. At first glance it seemed just like another large shard in the distance, but zooming, the profile was unmistakable.

It was a ship. The image quality wasn't superb, but there was no doubt it was the Scavenging Savant. It was also drifting quickly, like it'd been struck recently, and looked battered to the Brink and back.

He checked the radio recording but only found static. Granted, there was so much interference any reply might have failed to get through. And maybe they hadn't seen the rocket, external cameras being smashed.

Or simply, there was no one to see and no one to reply.

Lok checked the coordinates, plotted a course and set thrusters to full burn. Whatever Faldos' fate, he would find out.

Just as he set off on his new vector, he rerouted the rockets before launching. Their general course was the same, but their return point would put them at the location of the wrecked ship, where he'd be next. He did still need to find the Nulljaw.

• • •

THE BURNING LIGHT of the blowtorch flickered across Faldos' visor. Another metal plate drifted free of the starship's inner wall. He placed it on a stack of the plates Ardor carried. He sent the puppet up through the breach in the bulkhead. From that breach, the only light was a pair of welding torches spark on the other side. No searchlights and of course, no stars.

"Got enough plates up here, sonny," came Daley's slurred voice. The older merrow was welding plates onto one part of the breach with his own hands, while also controlling a puppet to weld another section. It was an impressive feat of multitasking for a man whose blood was mostly ethanol. "Need you up here to help welding."

"I'm comfortable in here."

"Look, sonny. Be a spacer long enough and you see strange and scary things. Still gotta do your job."

"You want me to just keep working like nothing's changed? The entire ship nearly got eaten by a monster! And let's not forget the shardstorm that almost finished the job it started."

"Storm could'a been worse."

"We lost two men, Daley!"

"Those idiots got themselves to blame for trying to steal the dinghy and run away. Learn from them and don't be a coward. Now come help me patch this place up in case of another shardstorm, or heck, your beastie comes back."

"If a shardstorm or that monster comes back a few slapped on plates are gonna do jack all, and you know it. Captain is keeping us busy."

"Maybe I like being kept busy. Means the boss doesn't mind how much I drink." There was a slurping noise of Daley drawing on a straw built into the inside of his helmet. "I don't know how you do it all sober, sonny."

"With steady hands."

Daley leaned down over the breach, shining his helmet light down.

"That's funny," The older Merrow said. "Come up here and I'll show you just how much."

"Like I said, comfortable down here."

An orange glow smoldered, lighting up the remnants of the engineering deck. Breff was leaning over a miniature core, ramshackled into the place of the original core.

"Well folks we may not have a working ship's radio but we got thrust back. It ain't much but it might let us limp to Ruby Roost."

"That's great, Breff!" Faldos said. "How long do you think we can be back?"

"At best five days."

"You're kidding."

"Nope. The Shroud is big, kid. And we'll be crawling."

"Since you got time," Daley said. "Quit bein' a pansy and get back up here. Took us forever to stabilize the ship long enough to crawl back outside and I'm not about to let the captain blame me for wasting it."

"I've already spent more than enough time outside that hull."

"Nothing's gonna happen. You only get one or two monster sightings in a lifetime. The odds of it happening again are-"

Black teeth closed over Daley, tearing the patchwork of metal plates like soft flesh. Daley's puppet was knocked downwards, nearly crashing into Faldos. He ducked and threw himself against the bulkhead, as far from the teeth as possible. Breff sprinted up the stairs and through the hatch.

The teeth bore down on the hole, knocking more plates loose, but not wide enough for more of the monster to enter. It pulled back and bit down again. It shook off bits of the hull like a spring hound ripping up a rag toy.

Faldos mustered his courage to follow Breff. But as he crashed against the door he found it locked. The man had actually locked it!

Ardor's laser could cut through it with enough time, but there would be so much light from the cutting. There'd be no escaping notice.

Faldos turned, crouching behind Ardor, for all the good that'd do.

The black body of the thing plunged down into the engineering deck. The teeth closed down around the minicore, extinguishing its light.

Darkness swept in. Faldos saw only the vaguest outline of the thing with the teeth. His breath sounded so loud inside his helmet. Though he knew the monster couldn't hear it, he still felt the need to quiet his pants and shrink his profile.

In the shadows the monster seemed to be tilting and turning, as if looking for something. And because it was so very very dark, Faldos could not be sure that those black teeth were turned towards his direction.

Yet he felt certain it was coming for him. The metal of the breach warped as the monster moved.

Blood blasted through his veins as his body ordered him to flee. But there was no escape. Faldos shut his eyes. He didn't want his last sight to be those black teeth.

# 5

# A SHOT IN THE DARK

---

**THE WRECK OF** the *Scavenging Savant* looked a bit like a beverage can Lok had used for target practice with his spreadshot. It looked even worse than in the rocket feed.

There were more holes and tears than there was unbroken metal. The biggest breach, a wide tear in the top deck, was unmistakably the work of Nulljaw teeth. The pieces missing from the satellite ring were certainly from the same culprit.

Other damage, like the scattering of small holes present on every side of the ship, seemed more like the collisions of thousands of shards at high speed. The ship's ashfield must've been down for a while. Another point against the crew's survival.

Lok felt his gut tighten up. That kid had better not be dead. He already had enough to keep him up at night.

He raised his cuff to his mouth, not taking his eyes off the display of the other ship, now only a few hundred meters from his own. "This is Lok Brightslayer of the *Hunt or be Hunted II*, contacting any member of the *Scavenging Savant*'s crew for rescue. Do you copy? Over."

No response. He hadn't expected one. They already failed to reply to the rocket's broadcast. He moved his ship closer, until less than a hundred meters spanned between them.

Lok slid his Twinshot off his back and checked the weapon. Loaded, of course. Safety was on. He flicked that off. He checked his second set of barrels, found them in good condition and returned both to his back.

He didn't put on a helmet and seal up his space suit. Lok didn't care for helmets. Dulled the senses. And the moment there was a breach, which happened a lot in his profession, you were basically done for.

Instead, he utilized three key devices to operate in the unforgiving void of space. All were retrieved from a locker within arm's reach of the helm.

The first was a small personal ashfield projector, to protect from any pieces of small fast-moving debris. A common tool for soldiers and spacers alike. It did interfere with guns, but he had an easy access switch on his glove so he could flick it off to fire at a moment's notice.

The second device, rarer, was a personal breathing barrier projector in the form of a bulky belt. Much like the one on his ship, it would keep a bubble of air around his body in a vacuum. But only three meters in diameter.

The third was a kalclaw, both a melee weapon and a grappling tool. One of the disadvantages of the portable breathing barrier was its interference with boost boots.

He strapped these tools on before casting his shadow cloak over it all. He'd look like little more than a silhouette to the untrained observer. A silhouette with a very big gun.

Lok moved to the hatch at the top of the cockpit. He hesitated, as one often does before plunging into a realm not their own.

He cracked open the hatch and climbed out.

The other ship was more tangible when viewed with the naked eye. The bits of pieces from its fragmented hull seemed so much sharper. Hostile. Its bent frame looked like it should collapse in on itself, although without gravity that was hardly a concern.

The dead ship wasn't fixing to get any more welcoming. Lok ascended on a cable up to the larger satellite ring and kicked, and before he had time to linger weightlessly, he thrust out one arm and shot the kalclaw's grappling hook across the gap.

The hook found purchase in the warped metal, connecting with a silent thud. Lok thumbed the cable retractor, lurching away from the Hunt or be Hunted II.

He'd make it across to the other ship in less than a minute.

And yet, in the few seconds he felt suffocatingly exposed in that empty expanse. The shadows, normally Lok's friends, seemed to eye him with hunger in this vacuous space. Bits of metal debris, like teeth, came at him in a cluster before being burnt up by his ashfield. With the hand that the cable wasn't sprouting from, he gripped his Twinshot like a vice. He swept the gun back and forth towards anything that looked like it might be moving towards him. But he didn't allow himself to swallow. He wouldn't show the void his fear, only caution.

He did allow a sigh of relief when he reached the end of the kalclaw's reel and was able to put his boots onto the *Scavenging Savant*'s ruined hull, locking onto the metal. He released the grappling hook from the hull and took the Twinshot in two hands, daring the void to send its worst at him now.

The void ceded him this round.

Lok moved across the hull. He found himself drawn to the big hole in the top deck. The one that'd clearly been bitten open.

Lok paused at the breach itself, examining the edge. Embedded in the metal was a kuron tooth.

He clicked on his Twinshot's flashlight and pointed into the hole. A shadowy deck inside. Not much visible besides a few floating crates.

Lok grabbed onto the edge and swung himself inside the chewed up starship.

He reached out and planted himself onto the nearest hard surface. In this case that was the ceiling. He strode along the top, shining gun's light down to the floor. The network of tubes, wires and roots, identified the place as an engineering deck. Near the breach, he found a burnt out core.

"So, that's how you got away," he mused. "Clever."

He turned away and walked down the wall to the floor. The nearest hatch was open just a crack. He crept over and nudged it open with his gun. A lightless corridor behind. Lok entered.

As he walked, Lok launched quick looks behind him a couple times a minute. One of the disadvantages of an air sphere was that it gave a false sense of security. It seemed like he could still hear and smell unimpeded, unlike in a suit, but the barrier didn't extend far enough for that to be practical. If he couldn't hear or smell something sneaking up on him until it was within a three meter bubble, it was probably too late.

Each time he turned, he found nothing but the shadows fleeing from his flashlight's glow. Yet his pulse still jumped and paranoia promised that this time something was there.

After about the tenth turn back, he once more found nothing behind. But when he looked forward there was something new down the corridor. Something moving.

The misshapen creature had too many limbs. Seven at least, and trailing cords that spilled out from the cracks in its shell. It sprang forward, a single bounce plenty to carry its skeletal body down the narrow corridor.

A subconscious part of Lok's mind, the part that didn't understand things like air spheres or gravity-free environments, quaked at the unnatural silence and weightlessness of the monster's advance.

Its arms were handless, ending in jagged blades that reached for him. Its single glowing eye burned in the darkness. The angry light cast shadows across its rippling armored body of cooled slag.

A monster of the void.

It's mistake was going after Lok. In a fluid series of motions, Lok disengaged his ashfield, dropped to one knee for an upward angle of fire and pulled the Twinshot's first trigger.

The stock hammered his shoulder in spite of the shock absorbers. He was nearly deafened and blinded by the blast that erupted from the weapon's barrel.

Most of the monster's upper torso stopped existing. The force of the kuron bullet drove it backwards and up into the ceiling, where it skirted across the metal, several limbs flying off. There was a hole in the bulkhead where the bullet had exited the monster's back. It was too dark to see, but if Lok were a betting man, he'd say the hole went all the way to the outside of the ship.

But he didn't relax, keeping his gun trained on what was left of the monster. Not a twitch. Just a slow drift backwards, no gravity to ground it. It was in pieces and the single eye in its head had gone dim.

Now that it was stationary, Lok could identify it as an electronic puppet, circuits bleeding out of shredded form. That did make his reaction slightly overkill, although he stood by his choice. Even if it wasn't a monster, it'd come after him. Speaking of, where was its puppeteer?

No sooner had that thought formed than his eye caught something darting away at the end of the corridor. Lok bounded after the blur, sliding around the corner, raising his Twinshot and...

Saw his 'target' spinning uncontrollably before it thudded into the bulkhead, at which point its body contorted with pain. The fellow had tripped. He was a Merrow judging by the number of arms and male by the anatomy. Suited up as he was, it was hard to determine much more. However, the six trembling hands he raised in surrender said enough.

Lok got closer and as he did, the lighting allowed a better glimpse behind the visor and the terrified eyes behind it.

It was a familiar face.

Lok's gut untwisted.

He let out a chuckle of relief and lowered the gun. He raised his cuff, transmitting over local comms. He said, as usual, what came to mind.

"Are you crazy, kid!? You trying to kill me with that puppet?"

"No! I...uh...sorry. Wait, are you not here to eat me? I thought you were a monster, honest. Scary suit you got on, what is that made of? Makes you look just like...a Skedwel Logra...oh. You're a Skedwel Logra, aren't you?"

"Master 'o observation, you are, Faldos. I see your dad's sharp edge skips a generation."

"Hey, you're not so sharp yourself, blowing up a perfectly good puppet when...Wait, how do you know my..." The kid turned his head, his whole body rotating as he did. "...Lok?"

"Good to see that university your dad put ya through was worth every coin."

"What are you even doing here, Lok? I haven't seen you since…the funeral."

"Yeah…"

Silence overtook them.

"…You came out here just to find me?"

"Something like that. You the only survivor?"

"Oh, no! There's a few of us, they just made the brave and daring choice of kicking me out here to see if that was more than just static we heard over our cuff radios or if the monster had come back. I had the puppet after all. Never mind, I pretty much saved all their sorry hides."

"Sounds like a stellar lot."

"Real class acts, across the board."

"Still, we can't just leave 'em to the void."

"I'll show you the way. They're holed up in the mess hall. Only got enough power left to keep one section lit and breathable. Even the ship radio's gone. Cuffcomps don't get a signal very far either."

"Makes it awful hard to get rescued like that."

"Pretty much figured we were ashed, yeah."

"Watch yer language, boy."

The kid actually rolled his eyes. "Yeah, yeah. So how did you find us?"

"Got creative."

"I see," he said in a way that sounded like he didn't. "Is there… more to the rescue team?"

"Just me."

"Oh."

"What's wrong, that ain't enough?"

"Uh, no. Never mind."

Lok couldn't deal with youngsters. Never could speak their minds. Or spoke them too much, in Sendro's case.

"This way," Faldos said before he kicked off the bulkhead down the corridor.

Lok followed.

"You'll get us out of here soon, right?" Faldos said. "After we're all gathered, right?"

"That's the plan."

The kid kept shooting glances at his Twinshot, like it was a nest of hivestingers.

"Is that a…gun?"

"Yeah."

"Wow. Never seen one in real life before."

"Ya need to get out more. You're dad never showed you any of his?"

"I didn't know he even owned any. Kept all his old hunting stuff locked up. It's not every day you see someone swinging around an old relic like that. Although I guess you always did have a thing for antiques."

"This antique turned your puppet into scrap metal."

"Ardor was in rough shape anyway. I don't mean to be rude. Trust me, I wouldn't wanna be on the other end of it. But it's not big enough."

"Pardon?"

"I mean, to the thing that wrecked our ship, I don't think that weapon would even scratch it."

"Hm. You got a good look at it?"

"Not really. But I've seen what it did to our ship."

"You lose anyone?"

"It got Daley. Two more ate ash before that. We lost our ashfield in the chase so-"

"Back up, how'd y'all get there?"

"We first ran into that…thing, while surveying a high-purity shard of kuron ore. Nearly ate my puppet, then nearly ate our ship. Nothing we threw at it worked and outrunning wasn't cutting it. We managed to overcharge the core to finally get away. Shardstorm hit a few hours later, ripping up what was left of our hull. Then it came back."

"How'd y'all survive it a second time?"

"That's the thing, I've got no idea. One second it was right in front of me, waiting to swallow me whole…then it just left."

"Just left?"

"How long ago?"

"Maybe an hour?"

It was possible the monster had missed the prey hiding in the remains of the ship. But Lok had a more likely theory: It'd smelled more prey coming and decided to hide among the reeds to see if it'd get another meal at this watering hole.

Lok suppressed the urge to tell the kid to move faster.

Faldos rounded a corner, taking them down a short path terminating in a hatch. He slid to a stop in front of it, tapping his cuffcomp.

"Well, did it come back again?" a voice came over local comms.

"No, but get this: There's someone here to rescue us! Old friend of my family's, if you can believe it."

"How 'bout that? Took 'em long enough."

The hatch slid open. A suited up Simacha stood to the side, an illsur drilldriver clutched in his four arms. He flinched on seeing Lok but shook off his surprise and lowered the makeshift weapon. Behind him, a stack of mess hall tables had been cobbled into a loose circular wall, from behind which the heads of other crewmen peeked out. They all either Simacha or Migdurs, no other Merrows like Faldos.

"So, you're our noble savior, eh?" the lead Simacha, probably the captain, said. "You got my thanks, sir. I'm Froll."

"Lok. And don't worry about it. Let's just get y'all out of here."

Cautiously, one by one the crew climbed out from behind the table barricade. Lok checked his cuffcomp. He just barely had enough signal to communicate with his ship, which was informing him that the latest round of rockets was starting to return. They'd need to take care boarding, so as to not end up between a rocket or...anything.

As all the spacers kicked out of the room, some patting Lok on the shoulder, others going for handshakes, and others simply drifting past with haunted expressions. The only one they waited on was Faldos, who'd gone back in for some reason.

"Kid, what are you doing back there? We gotta go!"

He moved inside the room and found Faldos at one corner staring at a pile of scrap metal. After a closer look, it wasn't scrap, but a beat up, grimy, old puppet.

"...it's a piece of junk, probably shouldn't even bother bringing it. Nothing like Ardor, the...one you broke."

"Look, kid, we gotta move..." Lok recognized a faded emblem on one of the puppet's shoulders. "Oh, it's a YottaWorks."

"You know something about puppets?"

"Not a thing. But I like their reelrods. Good products. Not flashy but they're durable and last long. They made a line of ships too...also good quality."

"Pretty sure this thing's been around since the Current Wars."

"And it's still working."

The boy scoffed. "For how much longer?"

A young Lok had said something very similar upon laying eyes on the used junker that was the only thing he could remotely afford payments on. How could a bucket of scraps replace the sleek Voidskipper he'd gone deeply into debt buying? How could it protect him the next time a juvenile Nulljaw came along and ripped his dreams of a bright future to shreds? Yet he'd bought that used junker. He hadn't really had much choice. Lok had many regrets in his life. Buying the *Hunt or Be Hunted II* wasn't one of them.

"You should bring it," Lok said. "Beggars, choosers and all that."

The kid sighed, but ultimately nodded. He reached down and strung the puppet's cable into his controller. With the tap of a button, the puppet jolted to life. With a few flicks of the controller, the puppet laboriously unfolded itself, all eight limbs, and a light blinking into existence on its face. It floated there, waiting for orders. Faldos guided the puppet ahead of himself as he finally made his way out of the mess hall.

The entire assortment of spacers drifted down the crowded corridor.

There was a ping from Lok's cuffcomp. The radio was meatier than most, so he still had just enough signal to reach his ship.

He checked the notification. All but one of the rockets had made it back. The reason for the ping was that the final rocket was late. Unless it had to make an unusual number of diversions…

Lok's gut said otherwise.

"I think we wanna move faster."

Proximity alarm. Something was approaching the *Hunt or be Hunted II*. He tried to pull up a live feed, but the video was grainy nonsense; too much interference. Lok pushed to the head of the group, having to shove the others out of the way. He was saving their lives, he had the right to a bit of shoving.

He came out on the engineering deck and leaped out of the gaping hole in the ceiling. Whirling he raised the Twinshot in the direction of his ship. Nothing was visible in the dust shade of the Shroud. Lok instructed his ship's searchlights to flick on.

Something was indeed approaching. Not yet much more than a black shadow. Frame of reference was tricky at this distance, but it looked almost as big as his ship. Less than a kilometer out.

Lok tapped away at his cuffcomp, ordering his ship to fire another miniature ship core from the catapult.

The glowing sphere blazed into the void, flying off just past the black mass, light dimming as the dust swallowed it.

The beast stiffened, hesitating between the larger meal ahead and the smaller one flying away. Its predatory instinct won out, and it turned to pursue the prey that was fleeing.

Lok let out a held breath. That ought to buy them another minute or two.

The spacers were gathering in the engineering deck below.

"What's going on up there?" the captain asked over comms.

Lok watched the black mass get further, its form obscuring in the gloom.

"...just get up here quick. We've got to jump over to my ship."

"You heard 'em boys."

A few at a time, they leaped up to Lok's level. They tensed as soon as they left the confines of the ship's metal hull. Wary glances were shot at the tooth-shredded metal around them.

"Go on," Lok instructed, motioning to his ship. "Aim for the top deck. I'll go last and keep watch."

After a moment to gather their courage, the first round, five men, jumped across the gap. Their suits sprayed gas to augment their speed, quickly closing the distance. In moments, all five had boots on the *Hunt or be Hunted II*'s hull.

Lok waved for the next group. The four spacers, including Froll, rose to his level.

Faldos, dragging his puppet, waved them on. "I'll just be a second, trying to get this thing's ashing thrusters working."

"Suit yourself," Froll said, before jumping with the other three.

They were halfway across the gap when the dark shadow reappeared. But this time, it'd come from another angle. It was pointed directly at the space between the two starships.

"Is th-that..." Faldos' voice trembled.

"Yeah."

"Am I seeing what I think I'm seeing...?" Froll asked.

"If you turn back now, you'll probably all die. Keep going. Soon as you get on my ship, make a break for the nearest hatch, there's one right next to where that Migdur fella is standing. Those of you already on the ship should do likewise."

The first five wasted no time piling inside. The shadow neared, drawn by the curiosity invading its realm.

The next four spacers touched down onto the hull and scurried into the hatch after the others.

Faldos' puppet started spurting gas, bobbing forward as it did.

"Oh, now it decides to work!" Faldos said, cursing the puppet as he reined it back in by its cable. He hopped onto the marionette's back, ready to rocket across the gap.

"Wait!" Lok pulled him back.

A shard shot out from the dark, passing over the top of the *Hunt or be Hunted II*, close and fast enough that the ashfield burnt away half its mass. It passed back out, flaking off glowing bits until it fully vanished.

A second shard flew towards the Scavenging Savant. Lok cursed, hit the deck and dragged the boy with him.

The shard hit. The entire ship lurched. The big shard broke into countless smaller ones, tearing through the space they'd just been standing. A sharp angle. Monster was on the move.

"What was that?" Faldos cried.

"Big ol' piece of kuron, I'd say. Our beastie just tossed it. Jump before it does it again."

"But—"

"Jump!"

The boy jumped, or rather, the puppet jumped and he held on as it shot across the gap. Finally, it was Lok's turn. He raised his kalclaw and fired the grappling hook, snagging his ship. With a jolt, he was hurtling back towards his ship.

They were halfway across the gap when a third shard shot out from the dark. This one came from behind. Beast was circling.

Lok was ready, though. If he timed this right then-

A panicked Faldos and his puppet jetted out of the way, slamming into Lok, sending them both reeling. The shard spun ahead of them, shearing through Lok's hookclaw reel in the process. The shard met its end when it wandered into the *Hunt or be Hunted II*'s ashfield and was subsequently ashed.

"Idiot!" Lok said.

"Well, we're alive, aren't we?"

"You didn't…never mind, Just take us the rest of the way to my ship."

"I can't. That was the last of his gas reserves."

"What?"

"I never use this puppet. So, I didn't think to top off his—"

"Forget it." With one arm he grabbed the kid and his puppet into a choke hold, with the other he aimed the Twinshot away from his ship and braced himself.

"What are you—"

Lok fired.

Angry plasma erupted from the weapon's second barrel, the kickback tossing them at the *Hunt or be Hunted II*. A rather girlish yelp came over the comms from Faldos.

Ashmotes danced around them, but they weren't going quite fast enough to be burned away. Lok considered, a bit late, that it'd might've been a tad risky move. But it beat staying in dead space with the Nulljaw.

They were nearing the satellite ring, but going too slow for Lok's liking. He tapped his cuff with his nose, prompting the ring to move into their path.

With finality they crashed into the side of the ring.

Lok sprang up, boots locking in place. He tossed the youth aside and removed the Twinshot's first set of barrels before slamming the second set into place. He drew a bead on the approaching shadow, now taking shape as a creature bristling with sharpened plates, and a burning tail.

He finger itched for the Twinshot triggers. As fun as it would be… nah.

Lok went back to his cuff and shrunk the ship's ashfield perimeter so it left the satellite rings outside. Next he switched over to the ring's weapons, all packing a far bigger punch than anything he could carry.

First, a magpulser. It'd send out an electromagnetic wave, pushing all ferrous metals away from the ship. It didn't work on pure kuron, but most of the shards contained enough iron for it to work. Damage wasn't the goal with the pulser, just to clear a way for the weapons that followed.

The pulser fired. Metallic dust caught up in its storm and washed over the black form like ice water. The dust swept past, leaving behind empty space. And the monster.

Sharpened kuron plates acting as both weapon and armor bristled out in rows. Two large spikes, one dorsal, the other ventral, were much larger than the others, pushing out from the rest of the bramble. It's body was thick, but not fat. Just powerful. Tapering to its rear was its tail that ended in an orange burning glow. Two smaller additional glows vented out behind the two larger spikes. Its bulky front end came forward in a blunt snout, wrapped in a solid shell of kuron.

Powered by the ship cores it ate, the beast was a living rocket with teeth.

And what teeth they were. The largest nearly as long as Lok was tall and even the smallest were bigger than his hand. The eyes weren't visible, and in fact Nulljaws saw slightly differently than most creatures did.

Lok started off with a volley of twenty cluster rockets. They erupted from a launcher halfway down the ring, burning their way across the black towards their foe, spreading out to hit a wide area.

The Nulljaw twisted on their approach, presenting its dorsal area where the armor would be thickest. The missiles slammed home, exploding with plasmic fury.

The dust cleared, the Nulljaw shook off whatever impact it'd felt, and pushed on towards his ship. Its armor barely looked scratched. Lok kicked his ship into gear, engine thrusting away from the Nulljaw. But they weren't accelerating fast enough; the monster would catch them before long.

Next the rotary guns. They spat a hundred lead rounds a second at their pursuer. The streams of burning ammo splattered and bounced off the beast's armor, as cleanly as drops of rain off a poncho. The Nulljaw might not have even noticed it was being hit.

"How ya like the taste of this one, then?" Lok muttered.

The pale blue distortion of the particle beam washed over the beast's skull. The barest hunt of grooves could be made off as the beam did microscopic damage to the metal. The beam pittered off to cool. The Nulljaw's noseplate was slightly etched.

A pair of coilguns next, powered directly by the ship's core, accelerating a kuron-tipped, tungsten payload at a kilometer per second. The two projectiles punched right into the Nulljaw's nose armor. Each shot left a noticeable, if small, dent in the creature's armor. It seemed momentarily dazed from the blow. It quickly resumed its pursuit.

"C-can we g-get ins-side?" a voice said.

Lok looked down, surprised to find Faldos still there. He'd almost forgotten about the kid. He turned back to the Nulljaw. It was gaining on them.

"Just a sec."

He fired one last weapon, another missile, this one a bit larger than the clusters. It arced toward the Nulljaw, following a specific path Lok set out for it.

It collided with the monster's skull and didn't explode but rather lanced into it. There'd been no explosive warhead on the missile, just a kuron tip. It struck one of the spots already hit by the coilgun. The Nulljaw actually lurched, twisting from the impact. As the bits of debris fell from its armor, Lok saw that the dent had gotten just a bit deeper. Progress.

Unfortunately, he only had one of those kuron rockets. They cost a fortune. The irony that he was currently surrounded by a field of kuron, even in its impure state, wasn't lost on him.

But the Nulljaw didn't know that and it twisted, breaking off from its direct pursuit to put some larger chunks of debris between them. It still followed, just at a zigzag. But that at least slowed it down enough for the *Hunt or be Hunted II* to get some distance.

Satisfied, Lok slung his Twinshot back over his shoulder, grabbed the kid with one hand, the puppet with the other, and slid on his boots down one of the ring's cables leading back to the ship. The kid unleashed a torrent of curses the whole way down. Lok landed gracefully enough, even if his knees did rock a bit more than they should've. He really needed to turn this ship's gravity down.

"Wha-what was that?" Faldos stammered.

"Getting down fast, thought you'd like that."

"I mean the part where you fired a sundering of weapons at that… that thing, with us hovering right in front of it like a snack!"

"First of all, those weapons are all that's keeping us from becomin' a snack. And second of all, if ya haven't figured it out yet, I ain't just here to save your sorry hide."

"What else could you be out here for?"

Lok grinned. "I'm a hunter of monsters, kid."

The boy swallowed. "Can you even kill something like that?"

Lok barked a laugh. "Ya need to get out more."

He marched inside, Faldos stumbling to chase after him, then stopping and turning back to bring his puppet.

Inside, Lok found the rest of the terrified spacers crammed in the main corridor. He brushed them aside, making for the bridge. Faldos, his puppet, and the *Scavenging Savant*'s former captain followed him.

The cockpit was already in combat mode when he entered, with a full three-hundred and sixty degree holographic display of the ship's exterior. The Nulljaw's form was highlighted with a yellow outline. A control harness had unfolded from the chair, which Lok strapped himself into. He could use the weapons with just his cuffcomp, but this would make for quicker and more precise firing.

Faldos hovered at the entrance, not doing much more than gaping. Froll starred as well, looking impressed but not surprised. He'd probably deduced what Lok's business was.

The Nulljaw was still following at a distance, keeping larger debris chunks between them. But it couldn't stay that way. Lok waited for it to pass out from behind another large piece, before firing the magpulser again. Once again, shards of rock and metal blew away from the Nulljaw, opening it up for another strike.

Lok fired off four small rockets, grouped together. To the Nulljaw, it looked like another cluster missile strike, and it once again twisted to present its thickest armor. That mistake was exactly what Lok had been hoping for.

The rockets split apart, but rather than explode across the Nulljaw's body, they each shot past, dragging between themselves a double layered net of charged illsur cable. The net encircled the Nulljaw, enclosing it as the rockets drew closer together again.

The monster thrashed in its snare, furious at Lok's deception. Its own thrusters burned, trying to push straight through the weave. But the net held, unimpressed by the Nulljaw's rage. The entire trap, rockets and net together were designed to slack, tighten, slow and accelerate as was needed to keep from breaking even under this beast's strength.

*Come on.* Lok silently urged.

Failing to break through the net on brute force alone, the Nulljaw turned to its greatest weapon: its teeth. The vacuous chasm of the Nulljaw's mouth split open, displaying endless rows of black teeth.

A targeting scope rotated out from the harness, sliding over Lok's eye, while a trigger on a joystick unfolded into his hand. A crackling hum went down the *Hunt or be Hunted II* as its strongest gun charged up.

It was called an ashcannon. A type of railgun running almost the entire length of the ship, firing a projectile bigger than Lok at four kilometers a second. The bullet wasn't kuron, but illsur. The metal wasn't particularly dense but it didn't need to be. It's conductivity and capacitive properties would let it be charged with ashen energy, the same stuff that protected the ship by burning up fast moving projectiles.

Pure kuron might've been somewhat resistant to ash energy, but even the Nulljaw wouldn't survive a direct hit of charged illsur right down its throat. If his aim was good, he'd skirt the bottom of the skull, pierce right through the core, and out back to the network of muscle strands. The slug would pass ashen energy onto everything it touched, burning the beast inside out. The one downside of the weapon was that the ship's own ashfield would need to turn completely off the moment it fired so as not to cause interference.

The Nulljaw was biting down on the net now, chewing through the first layer. In seconds, bits of cable under tension spilt out in all directions, slapping against the Nulljaw's armor in their death throes. That was one layer down. One more and the net was gone and the beast was free. It wouldn't get the chance.

The scope pulled over Lok's eyes and he gripped the trigger on the massive gun.

*Open your mouth.* he urged.

The Nulljaw started to open its mouth, but turned to thrash again. Bad angle. He needed to fire straight down its gullet. The Nulljaw turned back, mouth closed again. But it hadn't gotten a grip on the second net. It'd need to open again soon. Sure enough, the mouth did crack, slowly.

The trigger sat under Lok's finger, eager to be pulled. Not yet… not yet…not-

"Hey there, old-timer! Seems you found our beastie after all!"

The shock of that unwanted, unwarranted, unspeakable voice over the radio jolted Lok into pulling the trigger at precisely the wrong moment.

# 6

# A GREAT BIG ASH HEAP

**IT CAN TAKE** days to set up the perfect shot. And in less than a second it can all turn to ash. Sendro was excellent at making ash heaps.

His sudden outburst had thrown off Lok's timing. Even then, Lok might've still managed to land the shot down the Nulljaw's throat, were it not for the second part of Sendro's 'genius'.

The idiot chose that moment to have his eyesore of a ship emerge from the gloom, into the Nulljaw's view, prompting it to jerk towards this new challenger. Lok's shot slammed into the Nulljaw's side. Its body twisted around the shot, drifting backward as one of its armored plates broke and fell loose. Ash energy sprayed out in motes of light. Not enough.

It was a miserable consolation, that the monster quickly shook off, before tearing the rest of the way out of Lok's net. The Nulljaw retreated back to cover.

"Sendro, what in all Sorask are you doing!?" Lok demanded.

"Huntin' this beast, same as you. 'Cept I'm gonna finish the job."

*Strangling, that's what this kid needed. A good strangling.*

"Ya see," Sendro went on, "I wasn't finding much on my lonesome. After I saw your rocket fly by, I was caught by a notion that one of the other one's might've located our kuron-y friend here. So, I followed it back and here we are."

"You just screwed up a perfect killshot you ashing idiot!"

"Relax, old man. I'll show you how people from this century get it done."

Sendro's ship, the *Chopping Block*, launched well over a hundred ash-quarrels. Small, guided spikes of charged illsur, they struck the creature all across its nearest flank, shattering in flares of ashen energy. A peppering of ash-eaten scratches appeared along the Nulljaw's plates. It pivoted away from Sendro's ship as he fired the second volley. However, this time they curved around the monster, attacking it from the opposite side. This stalled the Nulljaw's retreat into the debris field. Sendro closed the gap.

Two massive, clawed arms unfolded from the Chopping Block's first satellite ring. The claws of ashen metal snatched hold of the Nulljaw's body. The Nulljaw thrashed in the new restraint, its own thrusters burning to escape. But with each buck and twist the ashen blades only burned their way deeper.

Weapons unfolded from the second of the *Chopping Block*'s satellite rings. First, a pair of ashen disc saws. Next, a pair of ashen drills. And finally, a pair of ashen chain cutters. Each of the weapons would be designed so that their speed of rotation would keep just within the threshold of an ashfield. Even with that limit, the oscillation would vastly increase damage. Sure enough, the blades shredded into the Nulljaw's armor, cleaving and cracking chunks of kuron off its body. The beast thrashed again, mouth opened and snapping futilely. Some part of Lok's psyche thought the creature should roar or snarl at its treatment. Yet this was space, and it struggled in silence.

"He's doing it," Faldos marveled.

Lok snorted. "Only thing he's doing is making a mess."

Every instinct of Lok's told him to charge forward, to stop this idiot. But he couldn't. Trying to get involved now would just make things even more chaotic.

Still, he brought his ship around so he was angled at the Nulljaw's mouth. He didn't have anything remotely resembling a clear shot, it was twisting about too much. The *Chopping Block*'s ashfield was in the way, anyhow. But if the moment did come, Lok would be ready.

Sendro's plan seemed to be to wear down a specific spot on the Nulljaw's armor, until he broke completely through. A decent enough idea. But his blades with all their moving parts meant he couldn't get them too close to each other, forcing each blade to 'take turns' slicing over the target spot. This shifting around between different weapons, making moderate progress, jostled the Nulljaw around and gave it just enough wiggle room. It got its mouth in reach of one of the arms that gripped it and bit down.

The mechanical limb twisted and contorted under the black teeth before finally giving up and snapping off. The Nulljaw victoriously chewed on the severed arm.

With only one arm now holding it in place, the Nulljaw's thrashing doubled in its violence. Sendro's plethora of rotating blades, earlier so effective cutting into a restricted target, now bounced and skirted off the monster's armor, unable to get a firm purchase.

The Nulljaw twisted around to lunge for the remaining arm. Desperate to keep this from happening, Sendro gave the Nulljaw something else to chew on and shoved the two drills into its mouth. A few dozen teeth broke off, but this wasn't the victory it seemed; the Nulljaw had hundreds. It chomped down hard, both drills grinding to a stop. The illsur drill bits held out a moment long before crumbling like foil.

But this pause had given Sendro a chance to unfold two more clawed arms from his ship to grab hold of the Nulljaw's body. These were smaller than the first, but the pair seemed to make up the difference.

"Ha! Thought it'd gotten the better of me, didn't ya!" the idiot's voice came over the radio.

"See, he's pulling through," Faldos said with relief.

"Oh don't worry, we've not yet reached the limits of Sendro's cranial density," Lok said.

The Chopping Block renewed its bladed barrage while firing off another volley of ash quarrels. This time the stream of glowing darts funneled down into a single point on the side of the Nulljaw, a crack where the broken claw had been gripping. The concentrated impacts widened the crack and left a respectable hole in the beast's armor. More armor laid beneath, but the plates would get thinner the deeper one went.

"All right, boys," came Sendro's voice. "Let's get at 'im!"

A Logra in a flashy red and blue armored space suit charged out of the ship, followed by ten others. They scampered up the ship's rigging, onto the ring, down one of the mechanical arms, and pounced onto the Nulljaw.

The flashy one, obviously Sendro, bore a ridiculously large axe that he brought down onto the cracked breach in the beast's armor. The image magnified, showing the young Logra throwing every bit of his muscled frame into pounding the Nulljaw's armor. He left shallow scratches in the kuron with each blow.

A laugh escaped Lok's lips. "He's a celestial idiot...but Malvit if he's not lacking in guts."

Faldos gaped. "Who is this guy? Some kind of hero from the songs?"

"He wishes."

The others joined Sendro in attacking the Nulljaw's weakened spot, while the ship's blades went to work on the Nulljaw's other side. They were gonna try and keep digging through the monster until they met in the middle. Still, even with all his efforts, Lok didn't see Sendro making much progress with just his own strength.

As if in response Sendro paused, his axe hovering. Maybe for once he'd make the right choice and pull back-

His armor plates began to shift, suit adjusting for the coming change. His arms rippled and expanded. His muscles seemed to almost inflate, growing thicker with each passing moment. Not just his muscles but the bones beneath too. Yet at the same time, his entire form grew more lithe, as if every excess was being dropped away in favor of pure unadulterated power.

"Uh, oh. He's goin' feral," Lok said.

"Feral?" Faldos asked.

"Guess a kid like you, born in peace, wouldn't have much experience in this. But Logra like Sendro and I have a card we can play when the going gets rough. It's called going feral. Basically, every cell in our body that can be spared is converted into muscles and bones. Makes us real strong and tough. Quick healing too. Also kinda turns ya into a great big idiot. So, in Sendro's case, there isn't much change."

Sendro let out a guttural roar over a comm channel he probably didn't realize was still open. He brought his axe down onto the Nulljaw's armor over and over, as if he could break through on strength alone. His compatriots followed suit, many going feral right along with him. Together they chipped away, bit by bit, at the Nulljaw's armor.

Such a simple tactic; that was typical of Sendro.

And though Lok was hesitant to admit it, there was a possibility that if they kept up the steady pace and nothing went horribly wrong, the young hunter might just prove victorious.

Something then went horribly wrong.

In Sendro's defense, not even Lok predicted it.

Some of the plates along the Nulljaw's flank rose up, trembling, jostled by something beneath.

Four new armored appendages shot out like serpents and grabbed hold of the *Chopping block*'s mechanical arms that gripped the Nulljaw's body. A magnified view showed that at the end of each of these armored tentacles was a spike-filled clamp. Like a mouth.

Lok stood bolt upright. "Sendro, get out of there! This Nulljaw's a Royal!"

"A what?"

The serpentine limbs went stiff, then thrashed. The ship's three arms cracked, joints warping unnaturally. Still the arms held on. The 'serpents' released only to snap back down again, this time locking their teeth onto the weakened joints. When they thrashed again, all three arms ripped apart.

The Nulljaw's serpentine limbs, called clutchers, went after the blades assaulting it next: Two buzz saws and two chain cutters. The clutchers gripped each below the blades, twisting them away from the Nulljaw body.

With nothing holding it back, the Nulljaw surged forward and bit down onto the satellite ring bearing the weapons. The ring shattered, saws and cutters spinning off into the void.

Still standing upon the Nulljaw's side, Sendro froze at the scene. His feral mind was probably having trouble sorting through what was happening. Or maybe he was just at a loss as to what to do, now that there was a storm of teeth and thrashing clutchers in between himself and his ship.

Lok was limited in what he could do. *The Chopping Block* was too close to the beast, its ashfield would interfere with any projectiles Lok could shoot. He only had a couple blades for close encounters and those wouldn't be enough to stop the Nulljaw.

"C-can't you do something?" Faldos said.

"Sendro's a drowning man. I go in now I might get dragged down, too. Still..." He wasn't the kind to watch even that idiot get eaten. "Whoever's helming the Chopping Block, drop your ashfield." Lok said over the radio.

"What? Why in blazes would I do that?" a frazzled voice replied.

"Because I can't shoot the ashing Nulljaw if you keep it up!"

"Drop that ashfield and you're fired!" Sendro barked. Apparently Lok's voice sparked angry lucidity back into his brain. "I can still kill this thing!"

"The Sundering you can!" Lok shot back.

Sendro ignored Lok. "Cover. I need cover. Jumping back to regroup."

Whoever was helming the ship swung blades on the second ring and started firing off volleys of ash-quarrels. The Nulljaw pivoted, pulling its clutchers out of chopping range and presenting its back to the oncoming quarrels.

The feral Sendro and his men ran back across the Nulljaw's body and jumped.

For a bone-chilling moment they drifted out over empty space, no cover, no protection. The Nulljaw noticed. A clutcher snaked towards them.

Again Sendro's helmsman proved his worth and threw forward the remaining ring bearing an axe. It slashed the side of the clutcher, not managing to cut it all the way through, but forcing it to pull back for a moment.

That moment allowed Sendro and his team to land back onto the hull of the *Chopping Block*. They landed in a dead run, sprinting for the nearest hatch.

Another of the Nulljaw's clutchers slipped past the blades and quarres to grab hold of one of Sendro's men. His claws scraped against the metal as it dragged him back towards the beast's mouth.

Sendro, turned on a heel and grabbed hold of his ally's arm with one claw and dug his axe into his own ship with the other.

Two other hunters moved to swing blades at the clutcher. That was when the second clutcher swept through, knocking the men aside and cracking into Sendro's flank.

Though several bones must have broken, his grip didn't.

Sendro's armor plates shifted under the mass of his trembling muscles, desperate to pull back his panicky, thrashing subordinate.

"Drop the ashfield!" Lok bellowed over the radio. "Or your friend is gonna die!"

"I—" Still that hesitation. But the helmsman almost sounded like he was ready to do as Lok said. But he hesitated.

And it cost them.

The Nulljaw ended the tugging match with Sendro when it surged forward and sunk its teeth down, shutting its mouth over the man like a castle portcullis. Unfortunately, Sendro's arm was stretched across the devoured space. The Nulljaw swallowed man, metal and arm in one gulp.

Lok watched Sendro rise, only to fall back, dazed. He wouldn't feel the pain for hours yet, not with his mind gone feral. The numbness, somehow, would be worse than pain.

A few of Sendro's men gained a fraction of their employer's early bravado and charged in to pull him back while the Nulljaw was rearing back for its next bite.

Sendro's helmsman tried to pull the ship back from the Nulljaw. But the beast had gotten a taste and now wanted the rest of the meal. With a fiery glow of its tail thruster, the Nulljaw shot forward, sinking teeth into another section of the hull. Meanwhile, its clutchers thrust into the existing hole, piercing and biting their way into the ship.

The ship's ashfield dropped, scattered motes of defensive lights fading away. Lok suspected this wasn't the work of the helmsman, but rather the damage the ship was taking. Either way, it opened the door.

Lok started out with a pair of specialized missiles. They shot out towards the Nulljaw, but instead of colliding, they fired off a secondary thruster at the front. The thrust equalized so that the Nulljaw was blasted with a constant stream of plasma exhaust. Blazerunners. Expensive. Effective.

The monster twitched with what might've been pain and retracted its clutchers back under its armor before its plates shut down flat against it. But it did not unhinge its jaw from Sendro's ship.

Lok studied his list of remaining munitions. He only had one idea to dislodge the beast.

He launched four of the H11 rockets. He turned on their ashfields. He directed them into wide arcs, so they wouldn't get too close to each other, or crash into Sendro's ship. The first one cruised just under the Nulljaw. Ash energy flared around the beast's kuron plates, eating them up at the edges. Minimal damage, but still a league more than most of his conventional weapons.

The Nulljaw noticed, twitching at its damaged armor. Another H11 flew over its dorsal area, ash again tearing a swath down its back. The third rocket took a small chunk out of its tail.

"Wow," Faldos breathed. "How are they doing that without even touching it?"

"Don't tell me you don't know about ashfields, kid."

"Of course, I do. They protect ships from anything moving too fast. But that- that monster is barely moving. It's just sitting there eating up the ship."

"Speed is relative, kid. Why do you think ashfields don't hurt their own ship when they're moving?"

"Because…because wherever the ashfield is projecting from is considered stationary. Which would be the ship?"

"Now you're catching on."

"So, from the perspective of the rockets…"

"…The Nulljaw is the one moving as fast as a rocket."

"Cool. Why didn't you lead with those?"

"This is a bleeding tactic. The Nulljaw's armor is too thick for the ashfields on those rockets to get all the way through, they'd short out. I use weaker weapons first to make it overconfident. I don't want it to run before I can get a killshot.

When the fourth rocket cut a thin rail along the Nulljaw's side, it decided it'd had enough, and lurched for one of the rockets. It missed. Barely.

The Nulljaw paused, seeming to consider this new threat. It turned back to the *Chopping Block*. With its teeth it ripped a piece off, expanding the existing hole, and started burrowing inside.

"Malvit, this is what I'm talking about. He's putting the ship in the way so I can't use the rockets without tearing it up too." Lok tried comms again. "Sendro, or your helmsman, or whoever's listening: You should abandon ship. She's as good as lost."

"N-never," came the ragged rasp of Sendor's voice.

"Stop being an idiot, you'll all die."

"We won't…" His voice faded, sounding distant.

"I'm afraid I have to agree with Lok, here," a new voice said.

It seemed the third hunter had also followed Lok's rockets.

K'val.

The Akadorn hunter's ship was neither bristling with blades like Sendro's, nor cluttered with guns and rockets like Lok's. Instead it was a simple, long cylinder with a single large satellite ring that had eight large mass drivers along it. While working on a similar

principle, the drivers wouldn't pack as much raw power as something like Lok's specialized coilguns. They did have the advantage of
being able to launch just about anything that fit down the barrel. In
a debris field like this, K'val would never run out of ammo. Judging
by the ship's shape, there was probably a much larger mass driver
built down the center. Worn painted letters on the side identified
it as the *Sling*.

"Seems you men are having a bit of trouble taking down this particular monster," K'val said.

"I was doing fine a minute ago," Lok said. "Mind running interference on the beast, while I pull this idiot out of the fire?"

"I have to decline, I'm afraid. I'll be going for the killshot, friend."

"Killshot? What in the void are you packing that could get a killshot at this angle?"

A hatch opened at the front of K'val's ship and the middle portion
of its cylinder body began to rotate. Lok was right about it being a
big mass driver.

"I'm glad you asked. See, I waited up a bit before casting off like
you two did. Got to know some of the locals. Might've slipped one
a few thousand coins to flub the inventory on a particularly potent
piece of mining equipment. Demolition."

The hair on the scruff of Lok's neck went stiff.

K'val went on. "Sendro, you've got sixty seconds to get your boys
off that ship. It hurts me to give you so little time, but I really can't
wait until the Nulljaw is done munching on your hull. This stands
the best chance of working if its mouth is still open..."

"K-K'val, wh-what are you talking about?" Sendro stammered.

"Sendro, get your men out of there now!" Lok barked.

"I don't take orders from you, old—"

"I think he's got an atomic bomb!"

Sendro's silence was telling.

"Ten points for the Skedwel," K'val confirmed.

"You'll kill them." Lok growled.

"I know. And that'll keep me up at night. But knowing I slayed a murderous Nulljaw that would've killed far more will let me get a wink or two."

"And I just bet the money won't hurt, either,."

"I…" Sendro's voice was uncharacteristically weak. "We're going. Just give us a few more minutes to get off the ship."

"I'm afraid you're down to thirty seconds, boy."

The Nulljaw ripped off another section of hull, not bothering to chew, just flinging it away and digging deeper with the next bite.

"This is insane, K'val." Lok said. "You know I can't let you do this."

"All right, fair is fair. You got it into position Lok. Half the pay is yours after I kill it."

"Money's not the issue, you ice-blood. What kind of—"

"How many people do you think this thing has killed in its life?" K'val said with surprising fury. "How many more will die if it gets away? You can call me cold-blooded if you like, but these monsters do not go down easily. I have it vulnerable, I have a rare weapon that can hurt it, I'm taking the shot before it gets to that ship's core and disappears back into the Shroud!"

"Sendro will—"

"We both know that boy made his bed when he decided to trade blows up close like a fool. And he also had an idea of the dangers when he started. We're hunters, Lok, and I've got a quarry to slay."

Lok found he agreed with some of the man's sentiments. Sendro had been asking for something like this to happen. The Nulljaw was unspeakably dangerous, and if it got away, it could be days or weeks before they tracked it down again. How many would it kill by then?

Accents along K'val's ship glowed as the mass driver got ready to fire. The nimbus of ashmotes around it fell away, in preparation for the shot.

"What are you going to do?" Faldos asked. The ashing boy was actually looking at him like he might have a good answer to the question.

People underestimate how easy it is to do nothing. But every day, dreams go unchased, opportunities unseized, heroics left to better, braver men. Even easier to do nothing, is when all you have to do to get what you want, deep down in your gut, is not so much as raise a finger.

Lok watched the Nulljaw tear apart a ship that was already lost. It was a scene he'd seen before. Once in reality, and countlessly in nightmares.

One shot and it would end. Lok didn't even need to be the one to pull the trigger. The rotations on K'val's gun reached their apex and they all were plunged into that heavy everlasting moment before the atomic bomb was fired.

The atomic payload was a bulky thing, never meant to be a weapon but instead intended to shatter massive asteroids for their precious compositions. It was almost certainly a shaped charge of some sort. Instead of an expanding chain reaction explosion like the bomb would work in an atmosphere, this instead would direct a devastating blast in one direction. Lok could see it all play out, the payload hitting the *Chopping Block*, detonating, the cone of energy ripping a hole through the ship and down the Nulljaw's throat on the other side.

Brutal, effective, lethal.

It'd be so easy.

Lok wasn't sure he'd ever done things the easy way a day in his life.

He fired the magnetic pulser.

The atomic bomb was shoved off course, spinning out past its original target to smash into a shard just as big as any of the starships.

Lok shut his eyes. Even through his lids, he got a general image of the expanding white-red cone of plasma.

When the light faded, he opened his eyes and witnessed the carnage of one of the most devastating "primitive" weapons ever crafted.

The shard was dust. Even now, razor sharp bits of it were burning up in the ashfield of the *Hunt or Be Hunted II*.

K'val had managed to throw his own ashfield back up in time and was therefore relatively unscathed.

Sendro's ship, without its ashfield, was another story.

Larger chunks had speared the hull, while the smaller one left hundreds of lacerations. Lok let loose another blast of the magnetic pulser, driving more fragments away from the ship. But did he actually save anyone inside?

The Nulljaw, its body contorted from twisting to avoid the worst of the blast, stretched itself back out, shaking out a few exterior plates that were too damaged to be useful, and turned away from them all, fire blazing from its tail.

"Malvit!" K'val swore. "Malvit, malvit, malvit! Lok, you idiot! What have you done? I've only got two more bombs and you'd better pray I don't use one on you!"

"Try it."

K'val's reply was something between a growl and a screech. "Why?"

"We're not monsters, K'val. We hunt them."

"Bah!" K'val engaged his ship's thrusters and chased after the Nulljaw, flinging explosive payloads at it with his smaller mass drivers

Lok instincts told him to chase too. But that was when one of the *Chopping Block*'s bay doors blasted open. A banged up shuttle limped out into open space. Someone *had* made it through.

He wanted to chase on, hunt this beast. But he couldn't. Too easy.

Lok instructed his rockets to come back before they went out of range. Then he turned his ship back towards the shuttle leaving the corpse of the *Chopping Block*. He moved forward to meet them. Lok snapped his fingers at the former captain of the *Scavenging Savant*.

"Make yourself useful and ready the bay for their entry. You might have to toss a few boxes out onto the deck to make room for the shuttle."

The Simacha nodded. "Aye, aye."

Lok sat back and sighed, running a hand through the fur on his head.

"What a day."

"H-hey, Lok?"

He turned to see Faldos clinging to one of the bridge walls with all six arms.

"Yeah, kid?"

"When do you think my eyesight might return?"

Lok stared for a second before barking out a laugh.

"You actually stared at an atomic bomb while it went off?"

"How was I supposed to know?"

"Common sense!"

"Apparently I haven't got much, otherwise I wouldn't be out here!"

"You crack me up kid...don't worry about your eyes. The ship has filters, so there won't be any permanent damage. Should start to see again in a minute or two."

"Well, that's something." Despite the humorous tone, the boy's body language was that of a puppet with all but one frayed string cut.

"Think you better take a rest, kid. Excitement's over anyway. For now."

"Good idea. Where's the bunks?"

"Only have a couple and the wounded will need those. But I got just the thing for you."

Lok popped open a nearby locker and retrieved a bedroll and tossed it at Faldos. It struck him in the side of the head and dropped to the floor.

"Hey!"

"Ah, sorry. Blind. Anyway, make yourself comfortable. I'm gonna go see to Sendro's crew."

"Lok?"

"Yeah, kid?"

"Thanks. You really saved us. Didn't really expect anyone to come, let alone you."

"Well, you're welcome all the same. But don't expect this to be a regular thing. Anyway, like I said: rest."

The boy swallowed. "And what if I can't after all that? After that... thing."

Lok recalled his own inability to sleep for almost a week after his first Nulljaw encounter. He went back to the locker and retrieved a bottle of amber liquid. This time he handed it directly to Faldos.

"What's this?"

"A man's drink. Don't guzzle the whole thing, but a little will take the edge off."

Faldos popped the top and took a sip. His face contorted and he gagged. "It's awful!"

"Awe. Would ya like a saucer of warm milk instead?"

The boy scowled. "At least my taste buds haven't been burned off from drinking too much of this engine fuel. Then again…" He blinked twice. "…my vision's starting to come back. Maybe the shock of the taste reset my system."

Lok laughed. "What a cure-all. I'll see about getting ya some real food and drink later."

"Will they taste as bad as this?"

"You're ashing right they will."

It was subtle but Lok caught just a twitch at the boy's cheek. It'd be a while before he smiled proper again. But it was a start.

Down the corridor some stairs and a turn brought Lok to the landing bay just as Sendro's shuttle crammed itself inside. The hatch popped open and the beleaguered remains of the crew piled out; ten of them. If memory served, that was about half what he'd started with.

Sendro came out last. He briefly met Lok's eyes before piercing the floor with his gaze.

"I suppose some gloating is in order." The younger Logra said.

"Nah. It really ain't."

Neither of them said anything for a moment.

Sendro broke the silence first. "Sorry…and thanks."

"Hm," Lok replied.

"I don't suppose you'd let me stay on for a bit and get revenge for my lost men?"

"No. Your time on this hunt is finished."

Both of their gazes naturally drifted to the space Sendro's arm had occupied.

"At least pay the ashing beast back for me," Sendro said softly.

"That I can do, son. That I can do."

# 7

## LICKING WOUNDS

**FALDOS HAD ALWAYS** wanted to live in the tropics. Like along the calm strip of Tropaka. Or to just disappear into the islands of Spiral Banks.

Getting a decent education and following a job in his field should have set him right up. But things hadn't gone that way. He hadn't been good enough, the jobs were fewer than promised and he'd been forced to do things he hated and live in miserable places.

Cold metal ships like the *Scavenging Savant* or the *Hunt or Be Hunted II* were the last kind of places he wanted to be, yet could never escape. Like gravity, he was always pulled right back down.

He'd come to the cargo hold but found little camaraderie in the kuron-eyed crewmen of both wrecked ships. He soon left it behind, his feet carrying him purposelessly down the corridor. He passed a bunk room, an armory and a workshop, not bothering to look deeper inside any of them.

It wasn't a very big ship and he soon found himself back at the threshold of the bridge.

"You don't have a single bottle of Argon Ale in this rusty can of a ship?" Sendro said, using his remaining arm to rummage through a locker, its contents spilling onto the floor. The Logra was still absurdly bulky from his earlier feral transformation and barely fit in the small bridge.

"Why would I stock something that tastes like drain water but costs its weight in illsur?" Lok said, oiling a harpoon blade. "You keep picking through my stuff and I'll break the only arm you got."

"Go on, old man, I only need one to toss you around."

"I don't need any to kick your sorry tail off this ship."

Sendro turned, flashing his claws and growling something in the Logra language.

Lok growled a reply and bared his teeth, stark white against his black fur.

On second thought, Faldos supposed his situation could be worse. He could be a monster hunter.

Sendro stared the older Logra down for a few more seconds before dropping his eyes. He muttered something about it not being worth the effort and shouldered past Faldos, nearly knocking him off his feet in the process.

Faldos stepped fully into the room, rubbing his shoulder. "He doesn't seem very grateful about being saved."

"Oh he is, Just not good at showing it. Manners are one thing I never managed to teach 'im."

"You used to work together?"

"For a couple years. He's young, strong and fast, and thought that was enough to compensate for not using his brain."

"Guess that finally caught up to him."

"I'd say. He lost more than just an arm back there. And his ego may never recover, though that'd be for the better."

"Maybe he'll also choose a saner career than monster hunting."

"Maybe." Lok sounded unconvinced. He got up, and stuffed the junk from the locker back inside. He paused at a knife with something engraved on the hilt, running a claw over it. He looked up at Faldos, eyes searching.

"What is it?" Faldos asked.

"...Nothing. Forget it." Lok stowed the knife and shut the locker. He returned to the captain's chair.

A question lingered on Faldos' lips. He decided not to ask. This wasn't the time or place.

"So, uh, do things usually go this poorly?"

"Not always. But more often than I'd like."

"And you still do it?"

"Do fish quit swimming? Does a springhound quit leapin'?"

"I don't understand."

An alert from navigation belayed Lok's reply. The old hunter consulted the console.

"Problem?" Faldos asked.

"Just a larger shard along our path. Need to move around it. Denser than usual. Might be the motherload you surveyors were looking for."

"No good to me now," Faldos said with a sigh.

"Why's that? If you mark the spot, you could come back for it later."

"Oh, I'm never coming back out here again."

"Not even after the Nulljaw is dead?"

"You really think that thing can be killed?"

"Ain't a beast alive that can't be killed, boy."

"Tell that to Sendro's missing arm."

"Hm." Lok kept staring at the readout. "Well, it doesn't hurt to take a peek."

Lok magnified the distant blob of the shard. While there was too much dust to get a clear view, its shape was distinctively odd for a shard of space debris. For one, it looked almost perfectly spherical.

"That's *interesting*."

Faldos swallowed. "Wh-what do you think it is?"

"Boring answer would be some abandoned garrison station from back in old Karlovus the Grand's time."

"Good, I like the boring answer."

"Or..."

"I don't like or."

"We could get closer and find out for sure."

"I really think we should just focus on getting back to Ruby Roost."

"It's not like we're taking a detour. It's right in our path, after all."

"I, um." Faldos swallowed, seeming to grasp for another argument.

"Live a little. 'Least we know the Nulljaw's behind us."

That was of some comfort to Faldos.

"Unless it already killed K'val and is onto tailing us." Lok added.

"You didn't have to say that part!"

"Yeah, but it's funny."

Faldos was really beginning to question the sort of men his father chose as friends.

*He saved your life,* he reminded himself. *At least indulge his madness a little.*

• • •

THE CLOSER THEY got to the great sphere, the clearer it became that it wasn't natural. A construct of intelligent hands. It also wasn't perfectly round. It had been once…until something cracked it open like an egg. And based on how its metal skin flared outward, whatever had broken it, seemed to have come from within.

The whole thing was pitch black, made up of millions of overlapping kuron plates. To call it bone chilling didn't measure up. Faldos felt cold in his marrow, in his cells. It reminded him far too much of the Nulljaw.

"What in all the cosmos is that?" Faldos asked when he could manage to form words.

"If I were a betting man," Lok said, ears twitching with what might've been excitement, "I'd say that's a Nihilian stronghold from back in the Current War."

"Nihilians? The void-breathers?"

"Yeah."

" Do you think there's any of them still here?"

"Don't know."

Neither spoke for a lingering moment. Lok rose from his chair.

"Welp, I'm gonna go take a look," He said.

"You can't be serious!"

"Course I am. I doubt it's a coincidence this thing is out here. It might have a clue where the Nulljaw came from. Maybe something I can use against it. Besides, how often do you get a chance to go poking around an eight-hundred year old Nihilian fortress?"

"Never!"

"Exactly."

"That's not a good reason!"

"What's the worst that could happen?"

"There's something in there that eats you!"

"Lotsa things have tried to eat me. I'm still here. Most of them ain't."

"Until one does."

"Better make it a good one, then, right?"

"No! Not right. If you get killed out there, what happens to the rest of us?"

"Fly the ship back to the station without me."

"F-fly back to the station?"

Suddenly the bridge was an even more daunting place.

"Yeah, you can fly a starship, can't ya?"

"...no."

"Really? How old are you?"

"Twenty-three."

"Stars, kid. You need to get out more. Anyway, just ask your captain to do it." Lok slid the Twinshot onto his back, already fitted with fresh barrels.

Insane. This old Logra was insane. "At least don't go alone," Faldos said. "Bring some backup, something."

"Who? Sendro? He's no good to anyone right now. The rest of his crew's not much better..." Lok's voice trailed off, then he smiled. "Then again, you might be right. I could use another pair of hands. Or maybe three more pairs of hands."

"No. no, no, no. You're insane if you think—"

"Relax. You can stay back here all safe and cozy-like. I just want to bring along your puppet."

"That is better. You're still crazy, though."

"Funny, your old man used to say the same thing."

"He was right."

"Yeah. But then he'd go and follow me right down into the Crustmaw's mouth anyway. Sometimes you just need someone else to be crazy first so you have an excuse to do the same."

Faldos didn't have a reply to that.

•  •  •

FALDOS DECIDED TO name the rickety old puppet, Graves.

It was twice as heavy as Ardor, had half as many sensors, and only one laser for diagnostics. The rest of the arms were packing tools like an adhesive spray or a plasma cutter. In short it was a crude workman marionette, for repairs and other dirty jobs.

He stood with Graves just inside the porthole leading out to the top deck of the *Hunt or be Hunted II*. He wasn't about to actually step outside the ship, although he did at least need to send the puppet on its way.

With the gravity off, Lok floated outside, his black cloak draped over him, shrouding all his weapons and tools so that his entire form became a silhouette. He turned his eyes, the only bright part of him, onto Faldos.

That visage had scared him as a child. He remembered finding excuses to hide when his father's big scary friend came by twice a year.

And that same big scary friend hadn't hesitated to plunge into a sea of black shards and battle a monster to rescue a kid he barely knew.

Life has a way of making you feel like an idiot in retrospect.

"Well? Ya ready?" Lok said.

"Yeah," Faldos said. "I think this hunk of scrap will fly."

Faldos tapped the primary thruster trigger on his controller, and Graves, connected by cord, rose slowly up from the ship. Lok snagged ahold of one of the puppet's legs, and both drifted up to the satellite ring.

Faldos checked the puppet's video feed. Graves had only one fat camera built into its head. The lens was old, a scattering of scratches blurring the image slightly. It was also tinted sepia. Whether by design or age, he couldn't tell.

They stopped once reaching the ring, already at the end of Faldos' twenty meter controller cable. Now things got complicated. Graves was an antique made by folks that were still scared of the metal monsters and their digital minds. The coding was very low level, to the point where he even had to control individual fingers when grabbing things. There were shortcuts around this level of overcomplication, but he was still figuring them out.

It wasn't particularly user friendly.

Aiming was also hard with the shoddy camera so it took a couple tries to get hold of the new cable. And a couple more getting it plugged into the puppet's second dataport. A bit more fiddling to lock the cable in place so nothing short of an ashsaw would disconnect it. As annoying as the process was, it was still far better than going out there to do it in person.

"Any day now," Lok said.

"This is harder than it looks."

"I'd sure hope so."

"Boy, it'd be a shame if this old puppet here malfunctioned and smacked you in the face."

"It'd be a shame if I had to climb back down there to stuff all six of your arms down your throat."

"Just don't hurt your back on the way."

"Don't strain your poor little fingers on that controller."

Faldos stifled a smirk. This wasn't like talking to the captain, who used threats like a hammer to pound his workers into place. Lok understood proper ribbing. A respectful kind of disrespect.

Faldos got Graves' fingers back around the first cable, the one leading to his controller. He pulled it out and the camera feed instantly went dead.

"Hang on just a second," Faldos said.

"I'll try to manage without ya."

He retracted the controller's cable, then shut the port door, making sure to seal it, just in case the breathing barrier were to fail. Then he ran back to the bridge, and plugged the controller into a console. He keyed into the ship's cable network and soon got a hard line feed from Graves back onto his controller. So nice to be on a ship where things worked. Even if it was an ugly hunting ship.

"All ready to go," Faldos reported.

"Now that I'm a year closer to death," Lok said with a yawn.

"Don't worry, I doubt you'll die of natural causes. Just look at what you're doing now."

"Could be worse. I could let a puppet do all the fun stuff for me."

"Could be worse. This could be my idea of fun."

Faldos activated Graves' main thruster, hurling both the puppet and Lok into open space. Flying was easier, just a matter of turning on the main thruster and occasionally tapping the supplementary ones for maneuvering. Ardor's still handled better. The sphere waited ahead, looking almost hungry, its breach opening like a mouth.

"Might want to get comfortable, Lok. You have almost a kilometer to go and Graves' thruster isn't the strongest. This is going to take a few minutes."

"All right, let's pass the time with a story."

"I don't know any good ones."

"Let's go with yours, then."

"Not much to it."

"That's what everyone says. Give it a shot."

Faldos decided arguing wasn't worth it. "Where to start? College, I guess. Before my dad passed, he had a fund set up so I could do whatever I wanted at university. I decided on Architecture and Structural Engineering in Space and Void Environments. Thought

I'd be designing habitats for people to live in, or maybe even an orbital space station like Ruby Roost. The stress made it feel like I was living under ten Gs. And I didn't even like the work as much as I thought I would. But I still finished up and graduated. I really tried my best to make it work so my dad's money didn't go to waste. But my resume ended up in an incinerator every time. Couldn't go back to Mom, don't think I could face her after failing this bad. So, I took this job telling myself it was just until I figured something else out. Still working on the something else part."

"They pay well out here?"

"Not at all. And they expect everything."

"You at least like what you do?"

"No. But at the time I thought it was something I needed to do. 'Sometimes you gotta do what you hate so you don't hate yourself.' Pops used to say that all the time when it came time to do something unpleasant. But I don't like the work or myself after this so I'm not sure what he really meant."

"Why not just go to work for yourself, then? Start a space engineering and whatnot company. Then ya get to do what ya like."

"Are you kidding? Where am I gonna get the money to start a business?"

"Take out a loan, ask for a friend to spot ya. Might be able to find an investor…"

"Doesn't matter. I don't think I really want to be a space engineer. I'm not very good at it. The scale of that stuff is…it's just a little too big for me. You make one wrong calculation, one flaw in your design and the whole project is a wash and you just cost the investor millions if not billions."

"So, if you don't want to be a space engineer what do you want to be?"

"Not a monster hunter," Faldos said with a laugh. But he did seriously consider the question for a moment. "I guess I've always liked working with puppets. Built a few small ones when I was a kid. I used to mod full sized ones in college as a hobby."

"So, why didn't you go into that?"

"There's no money in it. Every Merrow and their mother wants to make puppets. Barely anyone makes a crown, though, unless you're one of the bigger companies."

"You'd be surprised what people will pay for a handcrafted product. I buy a lot of my gear that way, since it can be more specialized."

"Eh. There's lots of guys out there better than me."

"Put in the work and that won't stay the same. Practice-

"-and hard work, sure. I heard that before. Easy for you to say, I'm sure you've always known you were gonna be a hunter."

"Nah, kid. I was a soldier."

"What? Really?"

"Yeah. Wanted to grow up and be a legendary hero like Karlovus and his Nine Knights."

"What happened?"

"Found out I don't like killing folks."

"Oh."

"Yeah. Got sidelined for insubordination and was discharged with all the honors of a wet sock. Wasn't sure what to do with myself after that. Until I ran into a beast that put things into perspective."

"Was it a Nulljaw?"

"Nah, I didn't run into one of those until later. This was a different kind of monster. Worse. But it's not a tale I feel like telling now. Ask me another time and you might learn how I got the name *Brightslayer*."

That served Faldos just fine. He had a negative interest in finding out what could possibly be worse than a Nulljaw.

Lok went on. "But let me tell you I didn't know my tail from my nose starting out. And in fact I lost my tail early on. I should've died, oh, hundred times or so. But I kept at it, practicing and finding folks to teach me."

"You knew how to fight already, though. That probably helped."

"A little. But you fight a beast different than a man. There was a lot of learning before I got any good. Helps if you find a friend to watch your back and add a little competition. That was your father by the way."

Faldos tried to picture his father armed with a Twinshot and laughed. "Still can't imagine him getting mixed up in this. Or maybe it's me I can't believe. That I'm related."

Faldos felt an unusual stab of jealousy at Lok. At this man who didn't shrink back at monsters. Stronger, braver and more experienced than Faldos ever would be. And he'd actually known his father.

Faldos wondered if his father had wished his son had been a more rambunctious child, who enjoyed their fishing trips rather than tolerated them. Maybe then he would've felt inclined to share with his son more of the side of him that slayed monsters.

"There's more of him in you than you think, I expect." Lok said, as if sensing Faldos' thoughts. "He was studying to be an industrial cable runner before a hunt of mine crossed our paths. He didn't plan it this way, either."

"The difference is I'm not gonna be a hunter at the end of this. It'll be a miracle if I go to space again at all."

"Funny you should say-"

Faldos cut off whatever Lok was about to say. "-Heads up. We're closing in on the sinister space station with the menacing tunnel you're about to go down into. Are you sure you like your job?"

"Kid, I consider it one of the perks."

The Sphere's breach spread out before them. Dark and deep, the lights from the ship didn't reach far. Faldos flipped on Graves' own searchlight. it revealed layers upon layers of rectangular plates making up the concentric walls of the Sphere. Many plates floated freely from when they'd broken off. In between the layers, the guts of the Sphere spilled out, cords and pipes like veins and arteries.

Faldos hesitated at the brink.

*It's just the puppet going in, not me.* And yet, Faldos had thought something similar when first exploring the shard that'd concealed the Nulljaw.

"Well?" Lok said. "You gonna take us down or do I gotta do this alone?"

When you owed someone your life, the least you could do was cover their back. Faldos' father wouldn't have stood for anything less, and he found that he wouldn't either.

With a tap of the remote in his sweating hands, Faldos lowered Lok and the puppet into the breach.

# 8

## NOT QUITE EMPTY

LAYERS OF BROKEN metal and twisted wire was all they saw as they descended. Faldos' initial impression of a hungry mouth shifted to something more like the guts of a carved up giant's corpse. This was a dead place. But not necessarily empty.

The walls fell away to an open chamber, the depth of which was not reached by the light. For a breath it was just Lok and Graves, lonely islands in a black sea. But from the shadows formed the hard lines of a metal platform. Faldos guided them towards it until Lok could seal his boots onto the 'floor', and draw his Twinshot. The weapon's flashlight flicked on, a cone of light spilling out.

Around them were banged up hunks of metal that might've once been spacecrafts. A landing bay, it seemed. Lok advanced towards the nearest craft.

Swallowing, Faldos moved the puppet after him. Every few steps, Lok would turn his gun and light to either side and behind. Faldos wished the puppet had a rear facing camera. The camera he did have wasn't much, but within a few steps, it showed him enough.

The vessel was mutilated with bite marks.

Lok ran a claw over one of the tears. "Looks like our friend was here. Chewed it up but lost interest. If there were any cores in these, they're long gone."

Lok moved on. They left the platform by way of a walkway that, rather than flat, was cylindrical, so any side could be walked on. It split off into other paths, and of course, Lok took the one that led deeper into the Sphere. Soon, they came to more layered walls, burst open by another violent breach.

Faldos swallowed. At least it'd been a straight shot so far. Grave's cable hadn't gotten caught on anything yet.

They arrived on a new platform, on one side of it a long console, on the other, a large capsule, easily the size of a landing shuttle. The body of the capsule was broken open, though the angle prevented them from seeing inside. Lok advanced towards it. The light crept around the breach, slowly stitching together a view of what lay within.

Even through a video screen, Faldos jumped when he saw it. Then, because the ship's gravity was off, he kept going up until he banged his head on the bridge's ceiling.

"Relax," came Lok's voice. "This one's dead."

Inside the capsule was a bundle of sharpened black teeth and plates, in the rough shape of a teardrop. But, rubbing his head, Faldos soon found that Lok was right. This Nulljaw was dead. And it was much smaller than the one they'd seen before. No flames burned from its tail, and a large portion of plates were missing, revealing a mostly hollow interior. The only things left was a lifeless sphere that looked a lot like a ship's core, and a lump of grey material stuck near the front of its skull.

"Wh-what happened to it?"

"Who knows? Might've gotten killed in battle and they brought it here to harvest the kuron. Or maybe one of its hatchmates killed it."

"What if there are more? Living ones?"

"Doubtful. Are you getting any readings of a ship core or similar types of radiation in here?"

Faldos checked Graves' instruments.

"No, nothing like that. Even Graves' sensors should be able to pick that up."

"Then we're probably okay. They wouldn't stick around here long. Nulljaws, living ones, eat ship cores to fuel themselves. Only way they can move as fast as a starship."

"What do they eat if they can't find ship cores? I mean, they're not machines, right? They must have some natural food source."

Lok stepped away from the capsule and started searching along the opposite walls. The light revealed diagrams of what looked like Nulljaw anatomy.

"Wild ones on the Black Reef usually feed off a creature called a starkrake which grows its own core. Failing that, they'd go looking for a sunsphere. Bit like a miniature sun. The Black Reef's a weird place."

"So, that's why it came after our ship? It just wanted the core?"

"That was part of it, yeah."

"But there's another part?"

Lok tapped on one part of the diagram. It showed one of those armored tentacles that the Nulljaw had used against Sendro's ship.

"Ones in the wild don't got clutchers like these. And while they can be angry ashers, they also don't usually go out of their way to go after folks like us unless you're stupid and poking your snout where it doesn't belong."

"What do you mean by 'ones in the wild'? Is the one back there not?"

"No. He's what's called a Royal. And he was bred for war. The snatchers are for catching crew members of a ship, or fighting a ship's defenses, like you saw. Royals also get a lot bigger, too. I thought our boy was full grown at first. But nah, if it was a Royal, I reckon the one we saw is young, not even half grown."

"You're saying it'll get bigger? No, wait, back up. What do you mean 'bred for war'?"

"It's a long story. You know about the Shaper Wars, right?"

"Been a while since history class. It was all about people scrambling to genetically engineer the best life form, right? "

"It wasn't just about trying to make the best life form. It was also about making the worst. They created living weapons. Monsters. Back in the day, they used shapers to alter life, making new species. Fought a lot of wars over the results. But all the shapers were destroyed along with the Starstriders during the Great Sundering. At least, that's what they thought. 'Til old Talovus the Son went and started a war with the Nihilians. Turns out the void-breathers had the one last shaper tucked away. Used it to turn the local Nulljaws into even worse killing machines than they already were. Nihilians even used it on some of their own, though that's a story for another time. I'm sure you heard it called the First Current War, but some folks think of it as the Last Shaper War."

"You think this shaper is here?"

"Nah, they destroyed that one at the end of the war. This was probably some kind of nursery. Grow the small Nulljaws into big ones and store 'em until they're needed."

Lok came into a new spherical chamber, this one smaller than the last, though still at least thirty meters to the top. There was tremble in Graves' cable, making Faldos flinch, but he turned to find it'd just scraped against a broken bit of wall. He hurried the puppet to catch up to Lok.

The chamber had a single massive capsule dominating it, a long console on one side with a scattering of small blinking red diodes. It was easily twice the size of the one in the previous chamber. And it looked like it'd properly been opened, no damage. Just split cleanly top to bottom.

"This, I reckon, is where our friend was, up until a little over a year ago."

It took Faldos a moment to follow his reasoning. "...When Scarlet Morn's two moons collided."

"Exactly. I betcha this fortress was buried deep inside of one of 'em. When the Nihilians lost the war, they left this place behind along with a sleeping Royal. I'm thinking there was a failsafe to let it out if the base was damaged. Or maybe just a bug in the machine.

Either way, the monster woke up seven hundred years after they put it to sleep and the only thing it knows is, it's hungry and it's made to kill. That's the nasty part about Royals. Most living things basically just wanna eat, rest and breed. Even predators usually only chase ya if they're hungry. But that ain't enough for these things. They like killing. They were engineered that way."

Faldos shivered. "Can we get out of here, now?"

"Just another minute." Lok stepped forward, inspecting the panel and the red diodes. "This seem strange to you, kid?"

"I don't understand any of the writing on it, but it's all void-talk anyway."

"Not what I'm getting at. Everything else in this place is dead, off. Why's this on?" Lok tapped on one of the diodes. Then tried flipping a few nearby switches. Nothing.

"I guess something in this station must still work, maybe it's plumbing."

"Doubt it." Lok shot one of his regular looks over his shoulder. "Oh. I think I just figured out what's still working. Turn that puppet's head around but try to keep still."

Lok's voice was calm, but his instructions were chilling. Faldos turned Grave's head, the camera getting a better view of the scene behind.

There were five of them, skittering around the inside of the sphere. The line between head and body was unclear. The pointed legs sprouted from a flared bundle of spikes, plates and cylinders tapering forward into a long stretch of metal that looked suspiciously like a gun barrel. Trailing behind the center mass was a frayed mess of wires and bits of metal. There were almost skeletal, hollow gaps in the metal spikes and plating across their bodies.

"Wh-what are they?"

"Vacgores. Shaped and cybernetically enhanced beasts altered by the Nihilians. Used in combination with Nulljaws for ranged attacks and boarding operations."

"Should I reel you back into the ship with Graves? I think I can manage it pretty quickly."

"I wouldn't. They don't seem to have noticed us yet. Sudden movements might set 'em off."

"How have they not seen? You and Graves are right in the open."

"Well, the good thing for us is the Vacgores are dead."

"What? I can see them moving."

"The biological part of 'em I mean. They're cyborgs without the 'org'. Probably never got into stasis like the Nulljaw, so their flesh eventually died off. Just the metal's left. No higher brain function. But their combat protocols are probably still online, so if we trigger that I reckon we're in for trouble."

"You can take them, though, right?"

"Not sure. Never tried it."

One of the Vacgores turned towards them, claws halting. It stilled, as if truly dead.

Then its legs pierced into the metal, bracing itself.

Lok shot first. Light flooded the chamber. A bullet the size of Faldos' thumb ripped the first Vacgore apart, metal pieces scattering weightlessly. The other four monstrosities launched into motion, jets of gas spraying from their bodies.

Lok's gun spat silent fire again. Another Vacgore turned to scrap and dust.

A third Vacgore landed about thirty meters away. It thrust claws into the floor and fired the gun at its nose. Lok threw his ashfield back up just in time for the bullet to explode into it, fragmenting into motes of light. Lok removed the spent pair of barrels from his Twinshot and started loading a second set.

A cylinder in the Vacgore's back shifted and it fired again. But the flechette that sprung from the barrel moved slower, the speed of an arrow. Lok dove to the floor as the blade ripped through his cloak, moving slow enough to pass through the ashfield.

Lok cursed and grumbled something about protocols and ash tech.

The fourth Vacgore landed on the wall behind them, locking down claws, a cylinder in its back shifting before firing a flechette at Graves this time.

Faldos let out a yelp as he saw the projectile fling towards him, piercing the puppet in its chest. An impact alarm went off. But Graves was unharmed.

The Vacgore targeting Lok shifted a cylinder again and fired a new projectile, an expanding net. He cursed, slashing his kalclaw as the net started to cinch tight around him.

The fifth and final Vacgore hit the floor and took aim at the old hunter.

On instinct, Faldos sent Graves bolting at the Vacgore to stop it. But at a dozen meters away, surely he couldn't reach it in time.

Either by accident or instinct, Faldos' finger found the button to extend Graves' arm. The limb telescoped outward, stretching out to latch onto the gun barrel. But too late, the flechette fired before Faldos could push it away.

But Lok simply leaned back, letting the blade shear through part of the net entangling him.

Faldos had to admit it was one of the slickest moves he'd ever seen.

The Vacgore tried to fire again, but Faldos managed to drive the barrel towards the ground this time, flechette finding only metal.

"Nice one, kid!" Lok said, slashing the rest of the net apart with his kalclaw. He dove to the side as the other two Vacgore opened fire.

Graves' Vacgore turned towards the puppet gripping it. Faldos did the only thing he could think of, which was to collapse Graves' arm back down to size, jerking the puppet in close, and punching the monster with another hand. The Vacgore was unphased. It pulled its own four spiked limbs out of the floor to stab Graves. four of the puppet's arms grabbed at the claws, three of them being caught, but the fourth slipping through to stab into Graves' chest.

Faldos expected the feed to die as the Puppet was torn up. But Graves held on. More impact alerts chimed as the Vacgore drove the claw deep into the puppet's body, anchoring itself as it would with the floor. Yet, despite a flare of alarms and reports of damage, the puppet's chassis was holding up remarkably well. With one arm holding the gun and another three holding back clawed legs, two of the puppet's hands were still free. Faldos quickly refreshed himself on the available tools.

The buzz saw seemed a good place to start. One of Graves' hands flipped over to the tool, a circular blade to cut into the Vacgore's armor. But the blade grinded uselessly against the black plating. Kuron. He was getting sick of the stuff.

The Vacgore activated its thrusters, driving them towards the end of the chamber. Graves slammed into the wall, back first.

*Impact warning: no significant damage received.*

This puppet really was sturdy.

Faldos cranked on his own thruster, pushing the Vacgore along the curve up to the ceiling. The Vacgore pushed back, their two jets fighting for dominance. It tried to inch its bladed legs closer, to nail more into the puppet's chest.

Faldos swapped the buzz blade out and used that hand to grab a spike-leg. This freed up another hand, one with a plasma cutter inside.

Flame arced out along the Vacgore's flank. But the flames did little more than the saw.

Unless…Faldos tried to stick the plasma cutter inside one of the gaps in the Vacgore's armor, but the Vacgore's legs could extend too, pushing its body out of reach. Worse, it was trying to get enough space to stick the barrel of the gun between them, with the business end pointed at Graves. He still held the barrel back but its superior leverage was starting to win out.

If it fired the main gun Faldos doubted even Graves, who had no ashfield, would survive.

He wasn't about to lose two puppets in as many days.

Graves was still on his cable. Faldos had the winch reel in a good thirty meters of line. Graves and the Vacgore were jerked towards the end of the chamber, thudding along the inside curve and crashing together. Graves was close enough to jam the torch into an armor gap, and cranked it to full burn.

The Vacgore's limbs twitched awkwardly, losing strength as something inside melted. Faldos kept the plasma burning until it ran out of fuel. By then, the Vacgore had gone completely limp, although with a leg still impaling Graves. Globs of metal and plastic drifted from the gaps in its metal husk.

Something bubbled up from his chest, leaving by way of his mouth.

Laughter, baffled, but also joyous.

"Yeah! How'd you like that? Come to a machine fight with me, you better pack something bigger!"

There were more Vacgores to deal with! He'd rip 'em to shreds, He'd...wait. He shook the adrenaline high from his mind. What had he just been thinking?

He wasn't a madman.

*Oh, right, Lok!*

He turned just in time to see Lok close the distance on one of the Vacgores, diving an ashen claw blade deep into an armor gap. A tug and he ripped out a chunk of circuitry. It fell over, ashmotes drifting from the wound. He dragged the metal body back up, using it as a shield to block the flechettes fired by the final Vacgore. Lok flicked off his ashfield, and with one more pull of his Twinshot's trigger, he ended the conflict with a flash of gunfire.

The Logra hunter turned to Faldos, or rather Graves, then to the Vacgore he'd felled.

"Nice work."

"I guess this puppet's not so bad." Faldos drifted Graves down to the old hunter. "Can we get out of here now?"

"Yes."

"Good." Faldos tried to jerk the body of the Vacgore off of Graves, but the anchored leg stubbornly remained in place. Lok moved over and tried his own hand at it, but the spike still didn't budge.

"Leave it," Lok said. "We'll tear it off on the ship."

Much as Faldos loathed bringing the thing with him, dead or alive, he didn't see a better option either.

"Kid, I think we've kicked the stinger hive," Lok said. He grabbed one of Graves' arms. "Start reeling in the puppet. On my mark."

Faldos saw it. The skittering shadows down the hall they'd come in from.

"What's the mark?" Faldos whispered pointlessly through the radio.

Lok hefted his Twinshot.

"Ah."

He took aim. The Vacgores were getting closer. Faldos' thumb hovered over the retractor button.

The Vacgores were almost in the chamber now. There were twenty, no, thirty of them.

Lok fired.

The silent projectile ripped through an entire row of Vacgores, shredding a half dozen of them.

Faldos slammed the retractor.

Graves and Lok jerked forward as the cable dragged them through the new gap in the Vacgore's line. Nose guns fired, raining blades. Like an umbrella, he stretched his arms over Lok, blocking the flechettes.

They broke out into the wider chamber.

Lok shouldered his Twinshot, flexing his kalclaw and bringing it to ashy life.

A pair of Vacgores materialized from the dark. Lok swung around the line like a trapeze artist and buried his kalclaw in the first Vacgore, dragging it to slam it into the second. Both fell away, left behind as the reel kept pulling.

There were more Vacgores crawling down the tunnel ahead.

Lok pulled another weapon from under his cloak. A handgun of some kind. He pointed it ahead of them and fired. Rather than a burning bullet like the Twinshot, a distorted blue beam escaped the gun, lancing down one of the Vacgore's nose guns. It exploded. He fired twice more, ripping off legs of two more. The other Vacgores jumped out of his line of fire, opening a slim path.

The cable was on a slight angle exiting the camber and Lok's side slammed into the metal as they scraped past the corner.

"Sorry!" Faldos said. Stupid, he should've used the jet to skirt past.

"Just keep pulling," Lok said through gritted teeth.

They came out in the main chamber. The Vacgores were waiting. They jetted towards them, firing a volley of flechette blades. Too many, Graves couldn't block them all.

Faldos fired Graves' thruster, pivoting them around the retracting wire, like a pendulum. They swung just out of the way of the blades, but slammed into the Vacgores. Most fell away. One Lok shot and kicked off of them. But another, knocked the gun from Lok's hand and put a claw into his leg. It dragged him off the puppet, both falling behind.

"Lok!"

"Don't stop!"

Lok fired his kalclaw's grappling hook, snagging Graves. With his freehand, he produced a long-bladed illsur knife that he buried in the Vacgore's midsection. It twitched as its insides were ashed. He pulled the knife out and cut through the leg claw, freeing him of the dead weight.

The swarm of Vacogores were chasing them now, and Faldos had to keep swinging them back and forth along the cable to keep flechettes from hitting home. Even more unwieldy was Lok dangling behind, kicking and slashing at any Vacgore that dared get close. Gradually he reeled his kalclaw in so he was again at Grave's side.

Light ahead or, above, the difference nonexistent in space.

The *Hunt or be Hunted II*'s searchlamp. Faldos got the impression of climbing up a well, or maybe out from inside a deep cave. But would they outpace the horrors behind? Vacgores were gaining. Worse, Faldos saw more gathered around the breach, pouncing down towards them.

Lok's next words carried the inflection of a smile. "Have your puppet grab me by the waist, I need both hands. Faldos did as he asked. Lok tapped his cuffcomp.

A Vacgore came close while Lok worked, but with a two-fisted swing, Faldos punched the monster back into the dark. For some reason, the following impact warning brought Faldos great satisfaction.

"Here we go." Lok said.

From the bridge, Faldos looked up to see the ship's satellite ring rotate to life.

The cold blue of the particle beam streamed down like water, cutting into the dark. From the bridge viewport, Faldos could see little, but through the controller feed…

A waterfall of distorted blue light washed over the Vacgores beside them. The monsters didn't fragment down into ash, like an illsur blade would've done. It was more like a pressure washer hitting a mound of dirt, washing it down a storm drain. The beam turned, so that annihilation orbited them.

All Vacgores around them ripped apart, though some still pursued from behind. Two blazerunner missiles fired from the ring, passing Graves and Lok. Rather than explode, they erupted with jets of fire from their fronts, burning a swath through the pursuing Vacgores, roasting them to slag. Faldos couldn't help but throw up a fist and whoop at that.

Graves and Lok were finally pulled free of the carnage and the sphere. Shortly after, the particle beam cut off to cool and the missiles ran dry of fuel.

"Think we got 'em all?" Faldos asked.

"Eh, I might've missed a few." Lok tapped at his cuff again.

Rotary guns fired from the ship's ring, lighting up the sphere's breach with bullets that ricocheted down into the pit. Sparks flew where they struck the remaining monsters. He fired one more missile, breaking up into a cluster of smaller payloads as it dropped. For a moment, they all went dark.

Then, fire. Orbs of violent orange erupted, filling up the breach until the plasma overflowed out of the sphere.

That same fire seemed to burn its way through Faldos' veins. He felt a pain on his face. He realized it was his cheeks straining from grinning too hard.

"Like I said," Lok spoke up, "It's one of the perks. Now be a lad, and get the med pack ready. It'd ruin my day if I lose a leg."

# 9

# A HUNTER'S SONG

**FALDOS LOOKED DOWN** at Graves, lying in Lok's workshop, with newfound respect. The puppet had just plowed through a storm of blades, was currently impaled by a dead cyborg, and most of its systems were still functioning. Still, they did need to remove said dead cyborg, hence the vice.

Lok had crimped the puppet into the biggest vice Faldos had ever seen, and then wrapped the Vacgore in cable from a spare winch reel bolted to the other side of the room.

"Ready, kid?"

He nodded. "Let's give it a shot."

Lok turned a dial on his cuffcomp paired with the winch.

The Vacgore body strained, anchored leg going taut. But it didn't come free. Lok turned the winch up higher. The winch whined, and the leg seemed to shift in its connection. But it wasn't out yet. Lok turned the winch up one more time.

For a moment, the stalemate remained. Then, without warning, the Vacgore ripped free of Graves, sailed across the room, and slammed into the winch, tossing bits of metal across the shop floor.

"Success," Lok said flatly.

Faldos turned back to the body of the Vacgore. "Probably be dumping that out into space now, right?"

"Nah," Lok said. "Never know when something like this might come in handy. That modular gun for example. And even an alloy of kuron is pretty sturdy stuff. I'm guessing it's at least fifty percent purity. Lot better than most hulls."

"Kinda gross, though, isn't it? I mean, it's a corpse…kind of."

"Kid, before we were smelting metal what do you think we made blades and bow strings out of? Bones and tendons. Even wood is made from something dead. A lot of stuff is when you get down to it."

"Guess that kinda makes sense. Still gross, though."

"You think that's nasty, you should see the Deathgaze body in my freezer."

"Think I'll pass. One dead monster is enough for today."

Faldos moved over to Graves and inspected the damage the spike had done. There was a coin-sized puncture hole in the chestpiece, with a craterous dent around it.

"I'll need to replace parts of the shell, and maybe switch out a few other components, maybe some frayed wires on the inside, but overall, he's fine. Walked away from quite the beating."

Lok looked over a suspicious gleam in his eye. "You know a puppet like that with a skilled operator behind it could come in real handy in my line of work."

"A skilled…oh no, no way!"

"You said you wanted to switch up your job."

"I also said I have no interest whatsoever in being a monster hunter!"

"You handled yourself pretty well back there. Granted you've got a lot to learn, but I'd say your instincts ain't bad. I heard from your other crew, if you hadn't jumped in when the Nulljaw first attacked, it probably would've killed everyone on that ship."

"That's not…I was trying not to die! I don't want to be in a line of work where I'm always trying not to die! Maybe nothing scares you, but this stuff scares the ash out of me! I may never sleep again after what I've seen in the past few days!"

"Easy kid, I was just floating the idea. Don't lose any fur over it."

"I don't have any fur," He grumbled.

"It's an idiom, kid. You really need to get out more."

"No, I really don't. And sorry, I didn't mean to uh…freak out."

"It's air in the void, kid. No worries.

Lok sat down on a nearby stool, and peeled up the black bandage on his leg. He injected another dose of healing tonic.

"Sorry about that," Faldos said.

"Eh. Scars are just stories on our flesh. And I've had a lot worse than this." Indeed, this close, without the cloak, he could see more scars on Lok, including a long one on his back and an even row of five along his lower gut.

"That's exactly what I mean when I said I don't have any interest in being a hunter."

"And maybe you're smart for that. It sure ain't for everyone." He closed the bandage backup and rose. "I'll be on the bridge."

"Right. I'll join you. Beats hanging around a dusty workshop"

"Aren't you gonna work on your puppet?"

"Later."

"You just don't wanna be around the Vacgore body, do ya?"

"I do not. It scares me a little, even dead."

Lok laughed at that. That simple act did remind Faldos a bit of his father. In a very annoying way.

• • •

THEY HADN'T SPOKEN much in the three hours since Lok retook the helm.

Faldos had spent most of that time hand weaving string figures, a calming habit he'd picked up from his mother, while he mentally shuddered at the idea of life as a monster hunter. Or rather, death, in the bellies of various beasts.

He struggled to picture his boring old dad ever doing this kind of thing. He did recall his father taking him to see a Rumbledrill leaper when the circus had come down to surface. And true, his father's primary hobby had been fishing, but that was a far cry from the madness Lok did.

Sendro stepped in, clawed feet dragging and scraping across the floor. His muscle mass had shrunk a bit since earlier as he shed the effects of going Feral. He was still far bulkier than Faldos could ever hope to be. He hadn't asked about the excursion into the Nihilian sphere. Hadn't even spoken since Lok had gotten back.

"How long until we get to port?" the young Logra asked, voice still a dull growl.

"At least another three hours." Lok replied, without looking away from the viewport.

"Mm." Sendro turned to leave.

"Ay! Since youse up, go grab me something out of that locker beside the door."

"Thought you didn't like me poking around your stuff."

"Special exception."

"Hm." Sendro popped open the locker in question, a sprawling mess inside. "What am I looking for?"

"Shadowstring case."

Sendro reached deep into the locker, not spilling quite as much onto the floor this time, before he came out with a black leather instrument case. He tossed it to Lok who popped it open and pulled out a midnight black, reflection-less instrument with glowing strings.

"What should I play?"

"'Death of a Hunter,'" Sendro said flatly.

"Too miserable."

"'An Arrow for You.'"

"Too bitter."

"I got nothing for ya, then, old man." Sendro turned to leave.

"I know! 'Wyre Cleaver'!"

Sendro hesitated, which Lok took as his cue to start playing.

"We all dream of slaying beasts,
Savin' lasses from monster feasts,
And gettin' kisses after it's ceased.
But times there's no monsters slain,
No lasses saved, no coins gained,
Not one kiss, but only pain.

And while life is cruel and life is hard,
There's a man who lived a life much charred,
Let's sing about the hunter with axe in hand,
Who from ruins became a hunter grand.

Slayer of monsters, Wyre Cleaver,
Brings his wrath down on all maneaters.
Killed beasts on every world and land.
The pearl in his axe, chopped from a Leviathan.

When Wyre Cleaver was just a boy, he became a monster slayer.
He found Frostbites, not one but three of the scaly flayers.
Set himself afire, to protect from their icy breath.
Chopped them all apart and laid them to their final rest.
And so he won, sporting burns across his chest.

Slayer of monsters, Wyre Cleaver,
Brings his wrath down on all maneaters.
Killed beast on every world and land.
He'll hunt 'em in void, jungle, crag, or sand.

Wyre was only starting, had his eyes on a Rumbledrill,
Up a mountain, chopping bits 'til he was nearly killed.
The beast gobbled up stone to rebuild, but t'was eatin' kuron ore.
Too heavy to move, Wyre swung through to the floor.
All that for no pay except for being gored.

*Slayer of monsters, Wyre Cleaver,*
*Brings his wrath down on all maneaters.*
*Killed beasts on every world and land.*
*Before his axe no nightmare can stand.*

*Next Wyre found a Guardian of the Trove.*
*He didn't care 'bout bones, it's for the monster he strove.*
*First he softened up the armored giant,*
*Dropped a comet on its head to make it pliant.*
*Three days they fought and three nights more,*
*Until our mighty hunter drove his axe into its core.*
*But of his limbs, he lost two of the four.*

*Slayer of monsters, Wyre Cleaver.*
*Brings his wrath down on all maneaters.*
*Killed beasts on every world and land.*
*Forged guardian's metal into a leg and hand.*

*So, even if there's no monsters slain,*
*No lasses saved, no coins gained,*
*And no kisses but only pain.*
*At least we'll know we're hunters and that's our story,*
*But hey, if I got a choice, I'll still take the glory,*

*Slayer of monsters, Wyre Cleaver,*
*Brings his wrath down on all maneaters.*
*Killed beasts on every world and land.*
*The pearl in his axe, chopped from a Leviathan!"*

Lok finished off the song with a climax of mounting chords, and then silence.

What a strange song. Why would anyone want to—

Sendro barked out a soft chuckle. "Thanks, Lok."

"For what?" the older Logra said, idly plucking at the instrument's strings.

Sendro paused, then laughed again, slapping his own thigh.

"You're right. I've been a disgrace."

"Won't hear an argument from me."

"Gotta pick myself up and work twice as hard. Just down to one arm, right?"

"Sure."

"You're a good man, Lok. Thanks for telling me what I had to hear."

"Whatever you say."

Sendro laughed again before walking off the bridge, humming the song's tune as he went.

"What is *wrong* with hunters?" Faldos said. He hadn't intended to say it out loud.

But Lok only scratched the fur at his chin and shrugged. "Lotta things, I s'pose."

"That song, about that Cleaver guy, why'd it make Sendro react like that? I mean, he lost an arm, but you sing a song about some guy getting chopped up and beat up and the message is that it's just 'the job.' What's that all about?"

"Not the point, kid."

"What is it, then?"

"Wyre Cleaver was one of the greatest hunters to ever live. If even *he* can't walk away from slaying unscathed, then the rest of us are in good company."

Faldos still didn't get it. He understood the concept, just couldn't wrap his head around the mentality of this profession. He intended to ask what madness made men take up this kind of work. A similar but very different question left his lips.

"Did my dad really do this?"

Lok side-eyed him.

Faldos went on. "Being a little outdoorsy is one thing. But did he really go creeping around abandoned space stations filled with freakish machines? Then sing songs about getting arms chopped off and launch missiles at monsters plucked out of a nightmare? My boring old dad?"

"There's two flavors of boring folk: The kind that were always that way and the kind that chose to be that way."

"You're saying my pops decided to stop being so 'interesting'?"

"Oh yeah. He was a riot back in the day. I'll grant he wasn't as crazy as Sendro there, but we got into some trouble."

"What happened to make him stop?"

"You did."

Lok's words hit Faldos like a sack of kuron.

Lok continued. "When you're young, brushes with death don't always seem so bad. He did slow down a bit after getting married, but still showed up when it counted. After a kid, though? That changes everything. He didn't wanna risk making you an orphan."

"For all the good that did…" Faldos said quietly.

"Yeah. Funny that."

In spite of a pension for cable swinging, Faldos' dad had been a boring parent to the core. Complete with bad jokes and a musical preference about a century behind. How else could a man spend a whole day holding a fishing pole over water? But in retrospect things that he'd thought were boring at the time were hints of the kind of man he'd once been.

Nothing made this more clear than the day he'd died.

The day of the collapse.

"Do you wonder?" Faldos asked. "If he'd still be alive, if he'd stuck with you?"

"Kid, I spent a lot of years learning how not to ask, 'What if?' I ain't about to start again. You can't know what could've happened one way or the other, any wonderin' is just pain."

"Do you miss him?"

"'Course. Not a hunter under the stars I trusted more than your old man."

"Was he any good?"

"He was an exceptional slayer. In all our years we never did settle who was a better shot, gun, bow or otherwise. And he had a mind for designing snares like you've never seen."

"Guess that was probably more interesting than the industrial cables he worked on after."

"It's like you said, gotta pay the bills somehow..." Lok chuckled, eyes full of memory. "We had this routine we did where he'd build some kinda crazy trap and I'd be the bait to lead the beast in. 'Course it didn't always go down that way. Sometimes the monster was a little faster than me, or the trap would go off too soon. Then it just turned into a slugfest." Another chuckle. "It's a mystery how we got out of some of those messes alive."

"But you still keep doing it?"

"It's fun."

"It's fun to almost die?"

"A little, but that's not the real fun part."

"Then what is?"

Lok took his time in replying, tuning his instrument for a moment before putting it back into its case.

"That Nulljaw out there. Have you had nightmares about it?"

Faldos swallowed but nodded. "Every time I've tried to sleep since it first attacked."

"Yeah. I was the same way. Still get 'em sometimes."

"But—"

"Most folks after catching just a glimpse of something like that, they'd go back to a home that doesn't feel near as safe as it did before, and try and forget what they ever saw. For better or worse, I never did learn to forget, or at least pretend to forget. Nightmares still come. That fear, that memory of being helpless of being...prey, is still there."

Faldos swallowed before asking his next question. "So, how do you sleep?"

Lok grinned. "By slaying 'em. There's nothing quite like looking your fear dead in the eye and sticking a blade right into it. To turn something hunting you into the prey. I do what I do, kid, because it's fun to slay your fears."

Insane. Every one of these hunters was insane...including his dad?

Faldos thought back to his battle with the Vacgore. Even filtered through the puppet, it'd been a bone chilling experience. The spike digging into Graves. The way it lacked any emotion, any fury, just cold violence.

But when he'd stuck that torch into its guts, when it'd finally shriveled up and died by his hand…well it hadn't been so scary at all, had it? That itself was underselling it. He surprised himself by how much he missed the thrill that overcoming the monster had given him. Even if Graves had done the heavy lifting, it'd been him pulling the strings. He'd faced off against a beast one on one and come out the better. In one moment he'd felt more in control of his life than he had his entire year as a spacer on a survey ship.

Lok seemed to notice the change. "There it is. The hunger, Looks like there's a little bit of your pops in you, after all."

"No I'm not a hunter, Lok. Never will be."

"Heh."

"Something funny?"

"Yeah. Your old man said the same thing the day we met."

Faldos tried to form some kind of reply, but instead just walked off the bridge. They couldn't reach Ruby Roost fast enough. He was taking the first ticket back to his homeworld.

First ticket back.

# 10

## CLEAN BREAK

FALDOS HAD EXPECTED a sigh of relief when he set foot back on Ruby Roost.

But for some reason workers in the hangar bay milled about on their duties, acting like the world was a relatively safe place to be.

He'd brought Graves with him. As far as he was concerned, the puppet had earned its keep.

The rest of the Scavenging Savant's crew shuffled off after him, led by the *former* captain. Finally within reception of local comms, the man started talking to someone excitedly, as if he hadn't also been on a ship being ripped apart by a Nulljaw.

Last of all, Sendro and the remainder of his own crew strode off the *Hunt or Be Hunted II*. The younger Logra marched with a stronger stance than before, his eyes sporting a predatory eagerness.

Lok stood at the top of the landing ramp, arms folded. He called down to the younger hunter. "This one was for free, but next time I'm charging a fare when you hitch a ride on my ship."

Sendro tightened his fist and whirled around. "Next time it'll be me pulling your voidy pelt out of the fire! Ya hear, old man?"

Lok nodded. "Be looking forward to it." He growled something in Logra.

Sendro growled something back.

They gestured to each other, what looked like a sign of respect. Sendro turned and walked away with his crew, a toothy grin on his face.

*Hunters,* Faldos thought with a shake of his head.

Still, he couldn't just leave.

"Lok?" he called up.

"Yeah?"

"Thanks. I...really have no idea how to pay you back."

"Forget about it. I owe your old man that much and more."

"You really came out here just to save me?"

"Or avenge you if you died."

Faldos shuddered. "That's morbid."

"This line of work often is."

"I can imagine. What's next for you?"

"Next, I go back out there and finish the job."

"You're really serious about going after that monster?"

"Deadly so. There's a beast that needs slaying."

"It took everything you shot at it! I'll admit you seem to be pretty good at this, but I don't know if even you can beat that thing."

"Remember what I said, kid? Some people can walk away, but I ain't one of 'em. I can't just forget. Long time ago, another Nulljaw ate The *Hunt or Be Hunted I.* I think it's about time I face this particular fear. And shove a rocket or two down its throat."

"You realize that eventually, one of these things is gonna eat you? If not the Nulljaw, then something else."

"Probably. Your Pops used to say he stayed around just 'cause he figured I wouldn't make it long solo. But everyone's gotta go somehow. 'Least for me it'll be interesting."

Faldos could tell arguing further was pointless. And maybe...a part of him did understand. Finally, he nodded to Lok.

"Guess there's nothing else to say but good hunting."

"Thanks, kid. Say hi to your mom, for me."

"I will. See you around, Lok."

"See you around, kid." He disappeared back inside his ship. Faldos turned away. And that was it.

What now?

He'd have to find a new job. Send out his resume again, ask what few contacts he had if they knew anyone looking to take on some more hands. And if he actually managed to find something, it was a roll of the dice how bad it might be. That prospect alone caused him dread.

But he'd go home first. Get his bearings and help his mom around the house. But…the thought of hopping on another ship and traveling out into the black suddenly didn't appeal to him either. Further, he wasn't sure he even had enough coin on hand to pay the fare. If there even was a ferry today.

He ambled over to Froll and other crewmen. At least he could see about getting his final paycheck. Just as soon as he'd stepped up to the circle of crewmen, the former captain let out a whoop.

"Good news boys! I kept the location data of that asteroid we found just before…well, you know. Management says that if it pans out, we're all looking at a big paycheck!"

There was a middling level of enthusiasm at that. Most of them were as jaded as Faldos. Some, more so.

"How long before the payout comes in?" Faldos asked.

"Just until a mining team comes in, verifies the finding and drill makes first contact. At the regular rate, probably a month or so."

Faldos thought it over. "No, I'm not sticking here that long."

Froll sized him up, but eventually nodded.

"Figures. Not everyone can hack it out here."

Faldos's eye twitched at that, but he let it go. "Just send my cut to my account."

"Sure thing, stringer."

Faldos wouldn't be surprised if he never saw a dime.

He turned to Graves. "I guess you'll be wanting the puppet back."

Froll shrugged. "I don't care about that rusty thing. Technically, I think it belonged to Daley. Seeing as he got eaten, it might as well be yours."

"Thanks." He said flatly. "Bye."

"Don't let the door hit ya."

. . .

"ONE TICKET TO Spinner's Orb, plus cargo."

"That'll be five fifty," The portly Simacha teller from the ticket station said.

Five hundred fifty was just about everything that was left in Faldos' account. But he could pay it.

"When's the ferry coming?" he asked.

"Thirty hours, hon."

He nodded. He could catch some sleep in the meantime and mentally prepare for the journey.

In short, he had nothing else keeping him here.

He turned to his cuffcomp and pulled up a transfer request to purchase the ticket with everything left in his local account. All he had to do was tap his cuff to the sensor on the teller's booth.

"Well, hon?"

Nothing holding him back...

Faldos shook his head and tapped the sensor. His cuff chimed, registering that the transfer had worked.

"Ticket's keyed to your cuff, you're all set, hon."

"Thanks...but, um..."

"Yes?"

"My room was in the company ship I worked on and that's...gone. Is there anywhere I can stay until the ferry comes?"

"Got chairs right over there."

She indicated the chairs lining the long ring of this section of the station. It was better than the floor. He strode over, Graves' heavy footsteps following behind. The two of them sat down. Faldos felt something poking him in the back. It wasn't from the chair. He opened a pouch on his suit and almost dropped the weighty object inside: a broken off Nulljaw tooth. Because of the reduced gravity, he'd forgotten he was still carrying it. He almost tossed it away just then. But at the very least, that much pure kuron was worth something. He stuffed it inside a compartment in Graves. At least it wouldn't be weighing him down.

He sat back and waited. And waited.

Faldos pulled out a thread to weave between his fingers. He hummed a tune as he twisted up string figures.

He stopped when he realized the tune was Wyre Cleaver. He stuffed the thread back into his spacesuit pocket and leaned back, crossing all six arms over his chest.

He closed his eyes, willing himself to sleep.

*Black teeth breaching the Scavenging Savant's hull.*

Faldos sat bolt upright, heart pounding against his ribcage. He forced down gulps of air until his pulse retreated.

Maybe he'd wait on sleep. He searched for anything at all to focus his eyes on, to distract his mind. He turned his gaze out the long window behind. There, he saw the bright surface of Scarlet Morn, the dead world they orbited. He watched miners further down the station dump heaps of metal byproduct down to the planet's surface. With little atmosphere, the artificial meteors would make it all the way to the bottom before pock marking the planet's face with their impacts.

Business as usual.

How long, he wondered, would the station hold up against a Nulljaw attack?

Hopefully, he'd never find out. Hopefully, the ferry would come first. Hopefully, Lok would kill the beast. Hopefully, he'd never see anything like the Nulljaw ever again.

Faldos found that he hated that hope. He was like a worm on a hook, wishing that no fish would come. He couldn't stop seeing himself as mere prey to greater, more powerful creatures.

*I can't just forget,* Lok's words echoed in his mind.

His mind once more went back to when he'd slain the Vacgore. From there, he let the current of his mind carry him to a related image. He pictured himself sticking a spear into the Nulljaw, watching it thrash and keel over, never to menace another starship. It was a cartoonish, wild fantasy. Faldos wasn't capable of such feats of strength.

But he knew someone who was.

Maybe…maybe he could at least be there when it happened. Maybe if he could just see the creature dead, it wouldn't haunt him the rest of his life. The same way other things had.

He thought of the collapse.

*The walls were crumbling around them, metal wires thick as arms snapping like string. He stumbled, fell, and had to be carried away. It hadn't been like the Nulljaw. He hadn't even fully realized what was happening at the time, just blind panic. His father set him down outside. Miraculously they were finally safe, free of the architectural coffin.*

*And then…his father smiled at him for the last time, before running back inside, towards the screams of people that were still trapped.*

Faldos had wanted to follow him, had told himself he was too injured to help. But it was really fear that had stopped him then.

His father hadn't said anything before he left, but his favorite phrase still echoed in Faldos' mind.

*Sometimes you gotta do what you hate, so you don't hate yourself.*

Faldos laughed in the hollow way a man does when he finally understands the words of his father.

He stood up. He pulled Graves up after him. Was he insane, considering what he was considering?

Some station workers ambled by, not a care in the world. They were worms on a hook too. They just didn't know it.

He started walking.

· · ·

*STUPID, STUPID, STUPID. Turn around now while you still can.*

These things kicked around Faldos' mind as he once again stood before the *Hunt or Be Hunted II*. He extended a foot towards the landing ramp, then pulled it back. Coward.

"What, uh, you doing there, kid?"

Faldos jumped, then turned to see Lok approaching, a large crate tossed over one shoulder.

"You...I thought you were on the ship."

"Resupplying."

"Ah."

"You forget something aboard?"

"No." Faldos took in a breath. "I..." he struggled, forcing the words out. "I want to come."

Lok set the crate down, put one clawed foot on it and leaned towards Faldos, inspecting him.

"Now, not an hour ago you as much as said you wouldn't be caught dead on a hunting ship again."

"I know, and just to be clear, I have no interest in becoming a hunter. I just want to be there when you, you know. Slay it. I want closure."

"What made you change your mind? I thought that we hunters are all madmen for doing this."

"You are. But as I sat there watching the station workers, I thought that an insane hunter might just be better than ignorant prey."

"I see." Lok scratched his chin. "You know I came out here to try and keep you outta harm's way."

"I know.

"And I don't know if your pops would've been happy with me bringing you back into it."

"I know. But I just can't help but feel like I'll always regret it if I don't see how this ends."

"Even if it kills ya?"

"No, I'd actually like to avoid dying at all costs."

"But you do want to come on the ship, which I'm gonna take to go fight a Nulljaw?"

"Yes. That doesn't make sense, does it?"

"Nah, I'd say you're finally starting to understand how hunters think." Lok stepped back, scratching a patch of black fur on his neck. "All right, here's the deal, kid. You stay on the bridge, should be safe there. Unless the worst happens and the hull becomes compromised due to an overabundance of Nulljaw teeth. That comes about, then you hop into one of the H11's. They're general purpose rockets, so they can work as escape pods. It ain't much but ideally the beast'll be too busy with me and the ship to notice ya. From there the rocket will take you to Ruby Roost, and we'll hope you aren't eaten along the way. Can't promise you'll make it back. What I can promise is I'll die 'fore I allow it to eat you first."

Faldos shifted his weight onto one foot, then the other. "Wh-what do you think your odds of taking it down are?"

"I'm pretty good at this, kid." Lok flashed a sharp-toothed grin. "I'd say we're easily at sixty percent."

Faldos stared at him. "That's all?"

"What? Sixty percent is good odds."

"Not by a lot!"

"If it makes ya feel better, K'val is still out there somewhere. If he's alive, he might soften it up a bit for us. Assuming he doesn't try to nuke everyone again."

"Well, what would that take us up to?"

"I dunno. Sixty-five?"

"Sixty five!?"

"For now. But here's the thing about hunting: it's all about stacking the deck. When we do finally face the Nulljaw, I am going to make sure it's the most dreadfully unfair fight you've ever seen."

Faldos still wasn't sure if he bought that, but it did sound better than sixty-five percent.

"Kid, if you're coming, come. If not, I got work to do."

Faldos entertained this last idea for an out. But in truth, he'd already made his choice. He rose himself up to his meager height, and tightened his grip on Graves' controller. "...Yes. I'm going with you. I'm going with you to hunt a monster."

There, he said it. It was happening.

"Then welcome back, Faldos. Since you're here, I think I might have some use for that puppet of yours."

"I take it you have a plan?"

"Plan might be a strong word. But it goes a little something like this..."

# 11

## GAME PLAN

---

"...SO, THE KID you went to all that trouble rescuing is now jumping right back into the Crustmaw's mouth with you?" The strain in Vosta's voice was obvious. The amusement was subtler.

"I didn't plan it like that," Lok replied. "But plans got a short shelf life."

"I thought you said you hate working with amateurs."

"No, I hate amateurs that think they're experts. Faldos is well aware he's an amateur."

"What difference does that make?"

"The former will argue with an order. The latter just listens. Most of the time, anyway."

He once again stood at the helm of the *Hunt or Be Hunted II*, cruising away from the crimson body of Scarlet Morn and the Ruby Roost station that ringed it. The midnight black debris field laid ahead, all the splinters and shards of rock, bathed in red light from the nearby star, looking for all the worlds like teeth and claws.

Lok had teeth and claws of his own.

"How long has it been since you had another hunting partner on the ship? Sendro left, what, two years back?"

"Three. And the kid's not a hunting partner. He's just here for the show. And maybe a little puppetry."

The ship drifted into the first thin layer of black dust. His visibility wasn't hurt much but Vosta's next words were warbled.

"Puppetry?"

"I'll explain later if any of it works."

"Fine by me. Just make sure you kill it, Lok. Otherwise I'm gonna have to find me a new hunter to leech off of."

"Just make sure you find me a simpler job after this one. Hate working in space. How about something planetside? Maybe tropical."

There was a warbled chuckle. "I'll see what I can do. Good hunting."

"Thanks."

The call went dead. Silence…broken ten seconds later by Faldos lumbering onto the bridge. He was fidgeting with a piece of string.

"I've never done this before," he said. "So, how does it usually start?"

"First we gotta find it."

"How? Fire off missiles until you hit something that's alive?"

"No, but you're not as far off as you'd think. It's tricky in a debris field like this. But I played with a few tactics the first time around, and I think I worked out a winner. Gonna fire off rockets with miniature ship cores on their noses. Those'll work as lures. Somewhere out there the Nulljaw's gonna sniff out those cores and come knocking. The rockets will follow a predetermined route back to the ship, and should bring the Nulljaw with 'em."

"What if the Nulljaw eats the core before it makes it back?"

"Then we'll know what happened when the rocket doesn't come back and we start searching in the area the rocket was sent to."

"That's clever."

"We'll see. Now come on, let's go attach those cores. And make a few other preparations while we're at it."

"Actually, could I use your workshop? I'd like to give Graves a few modifications."

"Sure thing, kid. Let's see what you got."

• • •

"PARTS." LOK POINTED to the wall of trays and drawers with a pile of trash at the bottom. "Tools." He pointed to a rack of power tools and other implements. "Bench." He pointed to the workbench. "Any questions?"

"Yeah," Faldos looked at the overstuffed tool rack. "Where's the impact wrench?"

"Third over from the top. Just above the sander."

"Ah." Faldos reached up, pulled it down and nearly fell over from the weight. He squeezed the trigger twice but a response wasn't forthcoming.

"There's an air hose attached to the bench." Lok said.

"It's not battery powered?"

"I got a battery one. But I need it for some work on the H11s. Besides, who doesn't like the nice hiss of air power?"

"Me. But I guess I won't be a choosy beggar."

"Attaboy."

Faldos had his puppet lie down flat on the bench. He powered it down and reached for the compressor hose. After only a couple attempts, there came the hiss and pop of the impact driver being plugged in.

"Oh right, I also need sockets," The kid at least had the decency to look bashful. "And one of those unpowered wrenches. You know, the traditional kind, without a motor or anything."

Lok stifled a chuckle. "Some people call it…a wrench." from a drawer he pulled out a set of sockets and a set of wrenches.

Faldos picked up one socket and stared at it.

"I used to work with puppets with my university's modular assembler. Twelve arms each with a different tool and auto-swappable sizes on everything. Even the survey ship had a crappy six-arm version. Haven't had to actually hold real tools in a long time. Not since…not since I was in dad's old workshop."

"How's it feel?" Lok asked.

"Greasy." Faldos slid the socket onto the impact, took a matching wrench, and with a deafening series of bangs, removed a bolt from one of Graves' arms. Faldos cringed. "Ear protection?"

Lok handed him some ear covers, which he got on after adjusting for his smaller Merrow head. Faldos took more bolts off until he could remove the entire metal panel on the puppet's arm. He started on the next one.

"You can adjust the torque on the side." Lok advised.

Faldos nodded, turning the dial with another hand. "I might need to dig into that scrap," he said. "Do you mind?"

Look waved a hand. "Take anything you need."

There was a tug at one of Faldos' cheeks. Almost a smile.

He requested other tools, which Lok handed over, Faldos taking them with his other arms while the first two still operated the impact and wrench. The boy became a flurry of all six limbs, dismantling the puppet as efficiently as a Grimeflayer dissecting a meal.

The requests for tools pittered off, as the boy's focus narrowed.

Lok smiled, seeing the reflection of another, now dead man, in Faldos. He turned and slid out of the room, unheard over the rattle of power tools.

• • •

LOK SET HIS impact driver down on the floor of the rocket bay. A glowing minicore was now set into the nose of five H11 rockets. They waited in their launch tubes.

Besides the rockets, he'd reloaded the rotary guns, the coilguns, and missile launchers. He'd also made sure his FL210, the largest harpoon cannon he owned, was serviced. And, of course, he'd set some traps inside the ship should the worst come about. The *Hunt or be Hunted II* was as ready as it'd ever be for another round with the Nulljaw.

He tapped his cuff, cutting off the ship's ashfield. Then the rockets dropped out from their tubes.

One after another, their tails erupted and they tore off into the dusty murk.

Bits of meteorite had already started pelting the ship like hail. Lok shifted the ashfield back on before more damage could be done. From there, bits of dark rock all flared orange before reducing to ash.

He climbed back up from the rocket back and returned to the workshop.

Faldos' six arms were a blur, each holding a different tool, winding, grinding and torching the puppet that was now suspended by wires before him.

"Faldos?"

No response.

"Faldos!"

The young man jumped and turned. Pushing welding goggles from his eyes. He smiled sheepishly.

"Sorry, I uh, got a little carried away."

"Let's see it, then."

Faldos stepped back, letting him take in the full view. The puppet had undergone a transformation, from an industrial implement to something deadlier. Deadly both because it was packing lethal weapons, but also because of its haphazard wiring and welds.

"So, I patched the hole in the chest with a bit of scrap metal. It's not pretty but I think it'll hold. You had a few old cameras and sensors sticking around so I installed those, since Graves was a little light in that area.

The arms I kept as a base, but I've been replacing most of the built in tools. From our perspective, in no particular order, we have the middle left arm where I installed a more powerful torch. You had a backup one that didn't seem like it'd had much use. Should be able to cut through a standard satellite ring cable in about two seconds. Bottom left arm buzz saw blade was already busted, but I saw you had some spare illsur blades, so after I swapped one of those in. I installed an ash generator in the abdomen and ran up contact wire. So, Graves will have access to both an ashen blade, and an ashfield. I, uh…can pay for all of this. Eventually."

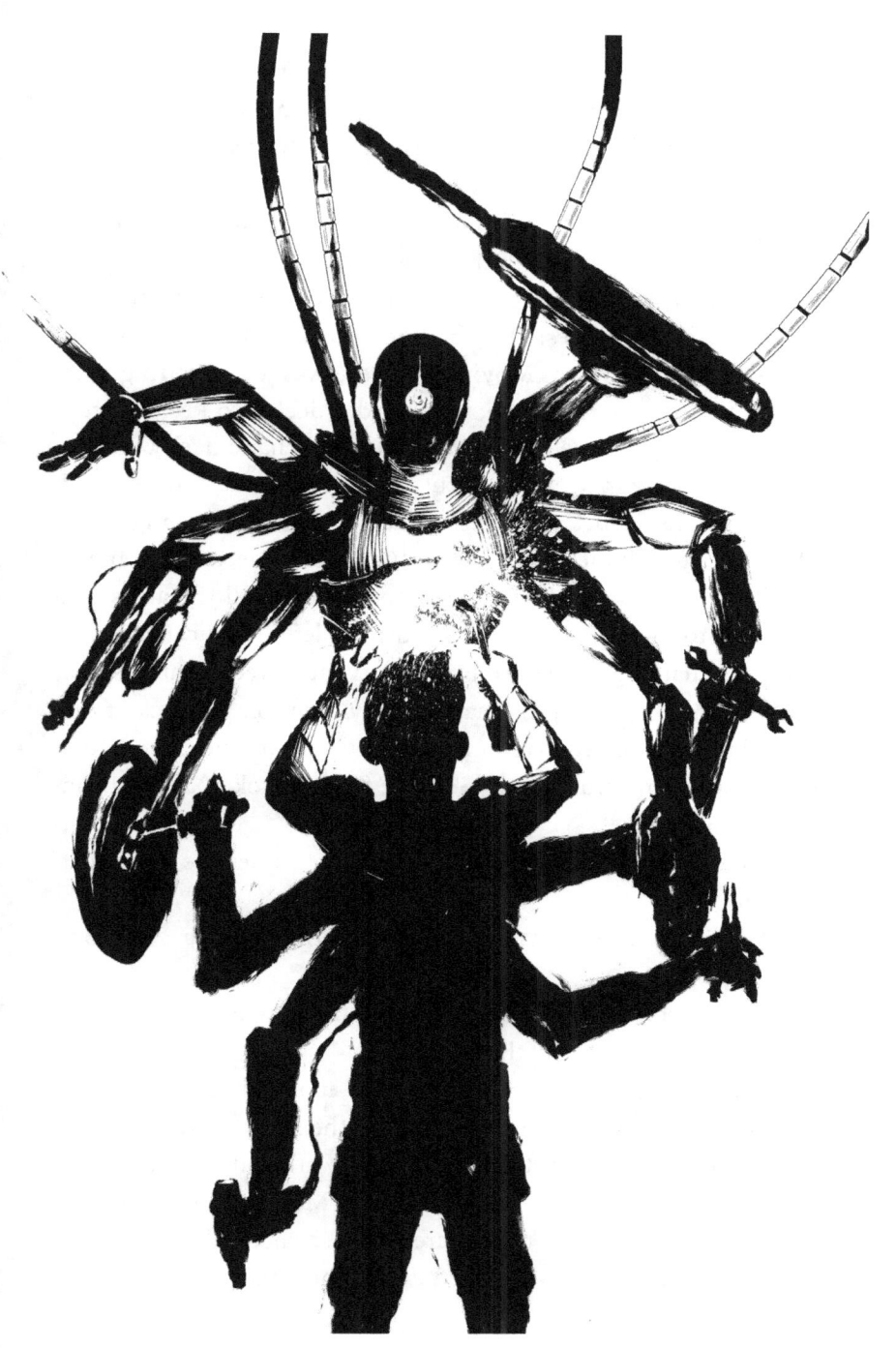

"Forget it. I needed to clear out this junk. What else you got?"

"All right, well here it gets a bit more interesting. The bottom right arm was originally a nail gun. I replaced it with…well the box said it was a micro missile launcher."

"The MM13. Forgot I even picked one of those up. Packs a decent punch for the size. Although the range is crap. Then again, in space, that's a lot farther than usual. Just…make sure the safety's on."

"I did. Several times. Only had one extra missile which I also stored in the abdomen. Moving on there was a fast-setting glue gun in the middle right arm, which I did decide to keep, since I thought it might come in handy, but since the hand itself was free, I've given it a high-yield laser cutter. Similar model to the one I had in my old puppet. It won't do much damage to anything made of kuron, but it'll melt most other stuff given time, and the range is potentially infinite. Finally…the top two. So, all the arms can telescope to twice their length, but the top left's hand can actually detach, remaining connected by a twenty meter reel. That was fine, I just needed more length. That bulky cylinder on the back of the shoulder is a new reel with a hundred meters of line. Also had a much more powerful motor. Got that from a broken angling rod you had back here."

"And to think I was gonna throw that out. But tell me about that top right arm."

"Ah. As you probably recognize…that's the modular gun from the Vacgore."

The weapon had been wrapped over the puppet's forearm and was larger than the rest of the arm itself.

"Almost threw my back out trying to lift it onto the bench. Kuron, man. But I got smart and had the jack do the hard work. Never did figure out how to access the weapon's software, but the gun had a mechanical firing mechanism built in too. Maybe the weapon was meant to be detachable, I'm not sure. There seemed to be some kind of safety switch, but uh…I melted it with the torch and it seems to work fine now."

Lok couldn't help but notice the flechette embedded in the ceiling. It wasn't the first time there'd been an unplanned weapon discharge on this ship, and probably wouldn't be the last.

"It's got three kinds of ammo: fast bullets, slow blades and expanding nets. I've managed to work up some wiring so I can switch between the three freely."

"What do I see here going on with the legs?"

"Ah, those. I pulled apart the Vacgore's claw legs. See, they each have an anchoring spike at the tip. I installed the spiking mechanism on the backs of Grave's legs so he can walk more or less like normal, but can also anchor himself when he needs to. Should let 'im cling to void-near anything. And it seems to be necessary when firing the main gun with the solid bullet, to keep from sending it flying from the kickback. And that…is about everything."

"Kid, I'd say you got yourself a huntin' puppet."

"I'd prefer if we didn't call it that."

Despite his words the boy cracked a smile at the compliment. "Still, even with all that, I'm not sure why I bothered. It's not like any of this will hurt the Nulljaw."

"Maybe not directly. But a few of these additions could help the plan go more smoothly. And options are especially good if things with the plan don't go smoothly."

Faldos nodded, still staring at the puppet, as if searching for places to cram in more devices. Shaking his head he finally turned to Lok.

"Did you fire the rockets?"

"They're on the prowl as we speak."

"Ah, so what's next?"

"We wait."

"For how long?"

"A while. You like card games?"

• • •

THEY DIDN'T WAIT nearly as long as Lok expected.

He'd expected to send the whole rocket set out at least two times before finding the Nulljaw.

Instead, they were in the middle of a card game when the fifth rocket made its first trip back, missing its miniature core.

Both sat up, scores forgotten on account of the fact that Lok had been losing.

The nose of the rocket had been torn off. But beam energy had cut it, not the tooth of the Nulljaw. That wasn't the only oddity. A fist-sized probe stuck to the side of the rocket. Lok didn't doubt both were K'val's doing.

The probe, once retrieved, had a video file waiting to be played.

Faldos sat beside Lok on the bridge, twisting a bit of thread between his fingers with anxious fervor. "Do you think he got it? Slayed the monster? Maybe this is his way of bragging?"

Lok doubted it. He played the video.

The camera was a first person perspective, looking out the viewport of a starship. As an arm with a folded wing reached forward to take the helm it became clear they were seeing through K'val's eyes, or near enough. Plenty of hunters favored helmet or chest cameras to document their exploits.

The forward viewport on K'vals ship showed the length of the vessel. The satellite ring was just visible, blasting its mass drivers at a distant figure ahead. Two other Akadorns worked to reload the weapons after each shot, zipping between them with the agility of creatures born to fly.

The Nulljaw's tail burned, along with the occasional flare from its dorsal and ventral thrusters. The beast's form was rendered silhouetted by the glare. It zigzagged between larger shards, letting them take the worst of the projectiles. Flickers of shadow suggested the clutchers at work, knocking away anything that made it past the obstacles.

The shards were more visible around them, ship lights carrying further through thinning dust. K'val was nearing the edge of the Obsidian Shroud. The space between the shards was growing larger, meaning the Nulljaw had less to hide behind.

Off to the side a new light appeared. K'val turned, magnifying the view until it became obvious that it was an H11 with a minicore fixed to its nose.

K'val let out a squawking laugh. He stopped when the Nulljaw turned its head near the new core. K'val unfolded a joystick from the helm, free-handing aim at the H11. With a pinpoint shot he blasted the minicore with a particle beam mounted on the satellite ring.

"Nice try, Lok, just a little late. But enjoy the rest of the show," K'val said to himself, turning back to the Nulljaw.

Ahead a light shone that had nothing to do with the planet or star. It was another minicore, attached to a familiar bulky object. Lok cursed, but with a smile on his face.

"What?"

"He was corralling it to his own bait. K'val's gonna try and feed it his other bomb. Shaped charge right down the throat. He's been chasing this thing, wearing it out of its fuel, all the while, he had his best weapon taking the long way round. And he stuck it to a juicy snack."

"Will that work?"

"I wish I could say yes, but…"

"…but this recording exists," Faldos finished.

"Yeah. But heck, maybe you're right. Maybe it's already over and this is him bragging."

Lok didn't believe it in the slightest.

They watched the Nulljaw race towards the poisoned core, hoping in vain that the impossible would happen. Instead, the improbable did.

A black wave of dense-packed, almost solid shards moved along the perimeter of the shroud.

"What is *that*?" K'val said.

The two deckhands hastily came down from the ring, slipping soon into the ship. There was a chittering of discussion between K'val and his deckhands but none of the three came up with an answer.

"Shardstorm," Faldos said softly.

Lok looked down. The kid wasn't occupying his hands with string figures or anything like usual. Instead he was just stiff.

"You have experience with these, right?"

"More than I'd like. I couldn't tell you exactly why they form, something to do with gravity fluctuations. Shards get caught up in the flow, gathering tight together and tear across the black. If you wanna call the Shroud an ocean, Shardstorms are a tidal wave. When the Nulljaw first attacked us, it didn't actually kill anyone. Not until it came back and ate Daley. But the shardstorm after? That killed two men who tried to run and battered the rest of us. Without an ashfield or a core to run away, we took the wave head on."

"I never saw one out there. They common?"

"Seems random. Sometimes you won't see any for weeks. Other times you'll get hammered twice a day."

Onscreen the Shardstorm had almost reached The Nulljaw and K'val's ship. The beast was still making for the minicore, but seemed almost reluctant now. Like it was considering the storm. It slowed.

"No! Just take the bait, ash you," K'val said.

It was easy to think of monsters like the Nulljaws as mindless killing machines. And while killing machines they may be, mindless, they were not. Many beasts could be shockingly analytical. Lok reckoned he was similar in that regard.

The Nulljaw was running the numbers on its potential food. The one ahead was nice and easy...but also small, barely a snack. Maybe too easy. The feisty one behind had been a pain to deal with, always staying out of reach to fire from afar. But it was a feast, a full size core, dripping with delicious radiation. And that wave of shards might just take the fight out of the prey.

But why choose? Both would be easy pickings inside the storm. The Nulljaw turned towards the oncoming wall of shards.

K'val cursed and hit a button on his cuff.

The bomb ahead fired its angry plasmatic stream, tearing into the Nulljaw's side. The camera overexposed white.

Just as things were coming back into focus, the shardstorm hit.

A wave of darkness swallowed everything. The ashfield flared, desperately holding back the torrent. It could only do so much. Shards of all sizes slipped through, burying themselves into the body of the starship. The satellite ring was broken into pieces, hanging by the threads of the rigging. The ship trembled and groaned from the impacts.

"Get to patching!" K'val called out. "I want those holes sealed! And find me a path out of this mess." A switch was flipped. Searchlights kicked on, but they pierced none of the darkness. The single working mass driver swiveled, and the main gun charged up. "Where are you...?"

The darkness grew teeth. The Nulljaw bit down on the hull. A shallow trench had been cut into its left flank from the bomb, glowing a soft orange.

K'val cursed, turning his last dangling mass driver towards the wound and fired. The projectile struck home, and the Nulljaw's body contorted in pain. K'val fired again.

The Nulljaw's clutchers sprang into motion. One knocked the projectile off course, while the other lanced into the mass driver, before ripping it off the broken ring.

The monster's mouth finally snapped shut, tearing a section of the hull clear off. The Nulljaw's clutchers next slithered into the hole. The beast bit down on another section of hull.

There was silence from K'val. Lok could feel him soaking it in, the dread of the predator-prey relationship switching roles.

Whatever courage lied in the man rallied.

"All right, boys! We've got one bomb left, that means one last shot to win! With me!"

K'val and his men rushed off the bridge, slipping down the gravity-less corridors. They ran down a side corridor into a room with curved walls and a large compartment. That'd be the outer chamber of the ship's main weapon, the gigantic mass driver. K'val slipped open the compartment, revealing a bulky object inside: the last atomic bomb.

The deckhands moved to pull it out, but K'val shooed them away, removed it and strapped it to his own back. Lok wouldn't have trusted anyone else with it, either.

They charged back out and down the corridor, where they met their writhing serpentine enemy.

K'val raised a gun. A Stroidstorm Light Bombarder. Despite the 'light' part of the name, it was nearly as big as K'val. A hefty under-barrel attachment unfolded, spearing into the floor to anchor the weapon.

K'val pulled the trigger and the gun's payload screamed across the distance, striking the nearest clutcher.

Not usually recommended for use in enclosed spaces, K'val was probably using the lowest possible ammo yield.

The camera still whited out from the blast. The clutchers didn't stop. K'val fired again. And again.

The serpentine black limbs came flailing. As they got too close for the Bombarder. K'val and his men defaulted to the ashblades folded up over their wings. In the chaos all that was visible was the sizzling of ash and thundering crashes of the kuron-armored clutchers.

From deeper in the ship, came the sound of screaming metal. The Nulljaw was chewing on the starship.

K'vals voice cried out. "Keep on it, lads! Gotta get the bomb to—" There was the sound of chopping and thudding. "—it's mouth!"

With a squawking scream one of K'val's men was grabbed.

"Vezal!" K'val grabbed his hand. The other deckhand lashed his blade against the clutcher's side to no effect.

The clutcher easily tore its captive out of grip and dragged him screaming down the hall.

K'val's voice again. "Hold on! We can still—"Another clutcher turned towards K'val.

K'val chanced another shot with the bombarder. No longer anchored, the kickback threw the hunter tumbling down the corridor as another explosion hit its mark.

Dazed from the blast the other deckhand stumbled blindly, making easy pickings for the clutcher.

"Noka!"

Both clutchers vanished down the hall and for the briefest moment everything was quiet, even the Nulljaw's chewing. The noise started up again and the clutchers, empty again, plunged back inside.

K'val cursed and fled. One caught up with him and caught hold of his wing. K'val fired again. The blast both broke the grip and threw him further down the corridor. But when he got moving again, he'd dropped the weapon and was holding what was left of one arm close to his body.

He slipped down to a lower hold of the ship and locked the hatch up tight. Boxes of supplies floated inside. K'val went to his cuffcomp and hesitated, watching an exterior camera's view of the Nulljaw chewing its way to the center of his ship. Lok didn't know the exact layout, but the beast looked close to engineering and the core within. K'val checked the feed from the shuttle bay. Static. The Nulljaw had eaten through it on the way in. It seemed K'val had no exit.

K'val's hands started to move again. He accessed his satellite ring, what was left of it. He found a probe launcher for tracking prey was still working. He took aim at the H11, still flying nearby, it's ashfield shielding it from the worst of the shardstorm.

Then K'val pulled the camera off his helmet and faced it. His helmet was cracked, his eyes tired in ways that only another hunter facing death understood. In spite of this, something like a smile touched the skin around those eyes.

"Well, Lok, guess I don't get the last laugh after all. I could try to fly away and live another day. But…out here, without a vehicle, in this shardstorm, with that beast waiting, I wouldn't last. I'd rather go out a little more…colorfully. He tried to laugh but the action seemed painful.

"L-listen up. I've got one bomb left, right here on my back. It might be close enough. But with several layers of ship metal between me and the Nulljaw, I doubt it. Let's not pretend like we like each other. But I think we both hate that beast out there more. So, if what I'm about to try doesn't work, then do me a favor and finish the job. Oh, and if you see Sendro, tell him it was nothing personal."

The recording went dead.

Faldos swallowed. "Do you think it worked?"

Lok pulled up the H11 rocket's own recording of the event. They watched it all play out from a more distant view. The shardstorm was waning, though the view was still grainy. They watched the Nulljaw dig itself into the ship, reaching for something glowing within. The core.

A small probe flew free of the ship, unnoticed as it attached itself to the observing rocket.

Then, the white blast ripped the ship apart and sent the Nulljaw tumbling end over end into the black. After an initial moment of stiff shock, the Nulljaw shook off a few outer plates that had been shattered in the blast. It didn't look particularly hurt.

Faldos' shoulders slumped.

The Nulljaw clawed around the wreckage for a moment, but finding no intact core, turned and drifted away into the black.

Lok turned off the recording. There was silence between them for a few moments before Lok decided it was probably up to him to be the one to break it.

"He wasn't a good man. But he was still a man. A hunter. And thanks to him we've got the location narrowed down. We'll avenge him like the others."

"Right."

Lok moved to the helm and turned the ship onto a new path, towards where K'val's ship had been destroyed. They'd actually be backtracking closer to Scarlet Morn. If the Nulljaw decided to go looking for food outside the Shroud…

He turned back to Faldos. The boy had a haunted look. Maybe Lok should have watched the video alone.

"H-hey, Lok?" The young Merrow finally said.

"Yeah, kid?"

"Do you still have that bottle of nasty liquor you gave me the other day? Because I think I'll have that drink now."

"Third locker on your right, top shelf. Should be some cups in there too. Limit yourself to two glassfuls. Just enough to take the edge off. I don't want you drunk when we find the Nulljaw."

"Gotcha."

"One more thing."

"Yeah?"

"Pour one for me too."

# 12

# THE WILL OF A PREDATOR

THE SHIP'S SENSORS sniffed out the beast by the end of the hour. Even in the Shroud there was a faint crumb trail of core-thrust.

Soon after they could see it. The dull orange exhalation of the Nulljaw's tail. The sight alone made Lok want to reach for his Twinshot.

Instead he flashed a sharp toothed grin. "We got him now, kid."

"Bet that's what K'val thought."

"You think we're gonna end up like him?"

"Do you?"

"Nah. K'val thought he just needed one or two good plans. But it's actually about having a lot of little plans to fall back on when the good ones fail. Besides, my ship is better than his."

Faldos only nodded and stared ahead.

Shards rippled out from the monster as it sprinted for the edge of the Shroud. Beyond it, the filtered light of the distant star shone over the shoulder of a large red circle. Scarlet Morn.

"It's going for Ruby Roost." Faldos said.

Lok grunted. "All those ships and their cores hanging around the station gotta look like hornhogs at a trough. It'd be a mighty big meal for that beast."

Faldos' six hands closed to fists. "Then it's gonna die hungry."

Despite the slight crack in his voice Lok was still impressed. He slapped Faldos on the shoulder. "That's more like it."

An alert flashed in the corner of the screen. Movement on radar. Lok focused the display on the area of concern. Faldos looked over his shoulder and let out a curse that made it clear that he'd spent more than enough time around spacers.

A wave of black shards was plowing its way laterally along the edge of the debris field, gathering up more rocky chunks and dust as it went. Another shardstorm.

The fur on Lok's scruff stood up.

"How long do you reckon until it hits?" He asked.

Faldos shrugged. "Maybe half an hour? Looks like we're on the edge of its path, but it'll still hammer us, even with an ashfield."

"Maybe there's a way to use it to our advantage. But let's still try to slay the monster before it hits."

Lok strapped himself into his combat chair, all the ship's weapons at his fingertips. The Nulljaw was still pushing onward. Time to get its attention.

He started out by firing off another core-tipped rocket. It flew past the Nulljaw, orange glow matching the beast's own, before sweeping back around towards the *Hunt or be Hunted II*. The Nulljaw pivoted its tail thruster, turning to face Lok.

Perhaps it was his imagination, but he thought it looked eager. As if thrilled there was still one challenger left.

The Nulljaw didn't push towards him with its thrusters. Instead it let Lok close the gap, while presenting its dorsal armor, where the armor was thickest. Smart beast. It was hungry, but cautious. Lok was too.

He found words on his tongue. "Together now, spear to tooth. Man against monster. And see who falls and who feasts."

Faldos turned to him. "What's that from?"

"Just a real old story."

Lok brought to bear the repeating guns and a volley of missiles, all squarely at the Nulljaw's dorsal plates. Barely scratched the kuron. The Nulljaw didn't flinch at such minor annoyances.

Lok's next weapon had even less firepower. The harpoon gun fixed in the turret on the bow. He pulled to a stop.

"Kid, it's time."

Faldos sucked in a breath, then with the flip of a switch on his controller, brought Graves online. The puppet was right beside the gun, at the ready.

Lok fired the first harpoon, trailing a cable across the black, lancing into one of the Nulljaw's dorsal plates. Graves loaded the next harpoon, one of five racked on the deck.

Lok fired again. Stuck it's forehead with the tethered harpoon this time. Graves reloaded.

Lok fired again. Another dorsal plate. Graves reloaded.

Lok fired for the last time. Hit the tail. Graves didn't pick up the fifth harpoon. That was for later.

"That…wasn't so hard." Faldos said.

"Says the guy with the easiest job."

The Nulljaw didn't seem to have even noticed its harpoons or tethers. Tired of waiting, the Nulljaw thrust towards its prey, mouth opening in welcome.

"You ain't gonna smile for long."

Lok launched four more of the H11s. The four caught the magnetic ends of the harpoon tethers as they passed.

The rockets made a wide arc before coming back around to the Nulljaw. Rather than collide with the beast, they looped around the beast twice, tangling it with the cables before all four cruised in the same direction, dragging the Nulljaw backwards. The beast twisted, trying to snap its teeth at the cables. When that failed, the clutchers came out.

Lok switched over to the quartet of coilguns. They fired in succession with each pull of the trigger. He pulled four times. The first three shots struck the clutchers. They were only glancing shots that carved bits of kuron armor off and prompted the three clutchers to retreat back into the Nulljaw's body.

The fourth shot missed entirely, and so the final clutcher locked onto a cable. He fired again, tearing a chunk of armor and black flesh off the clutcher. Not enough. It flexed and snapped off the cable. It retreated back within, before another shot could cut the limb off. One of the rockets flew free, but the other three remained, the cables holding fast.

Lok didn't panic. Three rockets should be enough. Should.

The rockets dragged the Nulljaw back around so its flank faced Lok. It's wounded flank, where K'val's bomb hit. Cracked plates overlapped the scar.

Lok pulled a trigger in his left hand, firing the particle beam.

Distorted blue light fell from the weapon, washing down onto the beast's scarred side.

The plates resisted. The beam wasn't the strongest of arms but it was precise. He couldn't risk damaging the cables.

The beam persisted. Small cracks widened. The Nulljaw twisted and thrashed, making it ashing hard to keep the beam in a specific spot.

But he never planned on finishing the job with the particle beam. That was just to soften his target up for the Ashcannon. He charged it up. It'd be ready in seconds.

The clutchers came out again. Lok fired, coilguns blasting. He was sloppier this time. First two shots missed, third just barely grazed a clutcher, causing it to retract. But the fourth, the fourth, struck the clutcher dead on, blowing a hole clean through it. The limb trembled with obvious pain. Lok fired again, tearing it the rest of the way off. The Nulljaw thrashed with agonized fury.

Small consolation. The other clutchers had cut two more of the cables loose before retreating. Only one rocket remained.

The monster flared its tail thruster, swinging in a waltz with the rocket and out of the Ashcannon's line of fire. It came in like a pendulum at the *Hunt or Be Hunted II*'s bridge.

Faldos yelped as Lok gunned the reverse thrusters.

The Nulljaw bit down on metal. But upon the ship's flank rather than the bridge.

The remaining rocket's drag on the beast was probably the only reason Lok had moved in time.

The Nulljaw's hold was shallow. All three of the beast's intact clutchers deployed, two grabbing the hull, and the final latching onto the satellite ring. Lok tried rotating weapons into place but the clutcher's hold restricted that.

The cable on the last rocket snapped free, releasing the Nulljaw entirely.

It unhooked its teeth and wound up for another lunge.

Lok fired the lateral boosters, slamming the side of his ship into the Nulljaw before it could bite down. The beast went spinning away until it pulled taut on its clutchers. Lok unfolded a ship-sword, ashen illsur metal on a long mechanical arm. He swung for the clutcher gripping the ring. The blade struck home, tearing a bit of black armor off the tendril. The Nulljaw released the clutcher, pulling it out of reach of the blade's follow-up.

No sooner had it released, than Lok shifted the ring so that one of the coilguns could get a line of fire at the Nulljaw's weakened side. The angle was still awkward, so the strike hit just above the scar, but it did the job. The Nulljaw turned and, using the clutchers, dragged itself alongside the hull so that Lok's own ship blocked its wound.

The Nulljaw bit down again.

Another shallow hold. It hadn't been able to get a good angle, keeping it's body parallel to the ship.

Lok flicked off that section of the ship's ashfield, then rotated the satellite ring to position a pair of coil guns down at the Nulljaw. But the monster grabbed the weapons in its clutchers before they fired. It strained to rip them off their brackets. The guns held for now.

But once more his line of fire was spoiled. He reached out with the sword again, but the Nulljaw used its third clutcher to knock the blade back. They dueled back and forth. He unfolded the second mechanical arm to add its blade to the fray. He tore nicks off here and there, but no solid cuts.

The Nulljaw chewed on the hull metal, not quite making it all the way through yet, angle was still bad. Lok didn't intend to give it a chance to get a better grip.

"Kid." He turned to Faldos. "I think it's time you went to try out some of your new toys."

The boy swallowed. "You sure?"

"A sword in its sheath don't cut nothing."

He nodded and sucked in repeated breaths. But he hadn't moved yet.

"You spent a lot of time on that puppet. Be a shame if you didn't show this beast what you got."

Faldos stood a little taller.

"Now," Lok added, "are you gonna do this, or do I gotta go out there myself?"

Faldos narrowed his eyes. "Stay in your chair, I'm going!"

His fingers danced across the controller and Graves skittered across the deck, trailing its ever-present cable as it slid off the side. Lok switched to another camera view, where the puppet slid between the starship's body and the Nulljaw's. A narrow gap of barely two meters. Graves braced itself against the hull and raised the Vacgore gun.

Faldos muttered something that might've been a prayer or a curse, then fired. The heavy slug hit the Nulljaw's weakened side right in the gap created by Lok's particle beam. The bullet buried itself in a cracked plate. The Nulljaw didn't notice.

"Ignore me, will ya?"

Faldos fired the missile next. The crack on the plate widened. Faldos opened it up with the plasma torch, edges of the kuron beginning to glow. He extended the arm with the buzzsaw, driving into the cracks to split them even wider. Finally he fired the Vacgore gun again. This shot pierced through the plate, tearing down to a deeper layer.

The Nulljaw's twitch was subtle, but apparently it felt a sting enough to reallocate one of its clutchers towards the insect nipping at it.

Faldos fired the puppet's thruster an instant before the clutcher slammed into the metal where it'd been. The faux teeth of the clutcher barely gouged the metal. Lok felt pride at his ship's resilience. The clutcher unhinged and sprung at Graves again.

Again the puppet rocketed away, narrowly dodging capture. At this point, Faldos reeled the puppet in full throttle by its cable. The clutcher made one more lunge, but Graves outpaced it and disappeared back down a hatch that slammed shut after it.

Faldos looked up, hands shaking. "Did you see that?"

"I saw."

"Did I really just do that?"

"Your puppet, but near enough."

"Did it work?"

The Nulljaw shifted position, but kept to its strategy of keeping between the ship and the ring. The beast was still deadlocking Lok's coilguns and had nearly chewed a real breach through the hull.

Faldos shoulders slumped.

"Hey now, you did well," Lok said. "He's nice and comfortable. Where I want 'em." To the Nulljaw he growled: "You like my hull? Why don't you get a bit closer?"

Lok brought two of the H11s back around. The fiery lances pinned the Nulljaw hard against the hull. The rockets kept pressing the monster even as their noses crumpled. The beast released the clutchers from the ring and knocked the rockets off.

But that left the coilguns free.

Lok fired. Again and again. The high density slugs did almost as well as the rockets at keeping the Nulljaw sandwiched against the hull. Even better, the armor plates were beginning to crack under the assault.

But the guns were running low on ammo. He had two more coilguns on the other side of the ring that were still almost full. He'd need to rotate the ring to place them. It'd only take a second or two.

The instant the last bullet fired, Lok spun the ring. He was almost fast enough. Almost.

In the brief respite the Nulljaw made a rocketing sprint away from the starship. Lok got a few shots off as it fled, but no solid hits. It hadn't been a complete breach but the beast left a deep bite-shaped gash in the *Hunt Or Be Hunted II*.

Lok would pay it back tenfold.

He thought the Nulljaw might simply flee. But instead, it darted towards a nearby shard. The shard wasn't nearly big enough to hide behind. What was it up to...?

The Nulljaw opened its mouth and swallowed the shard.

It turned back to face the *Hunt Or Be Hunted II*. Something behind its teeth glowed. Lok had an idea of what would happen next. He calculated his response.

Nulljaw opened its maw and spewed a ball of molten metal.

Lok didn't expand the ashfield in time. The molten projectile ripped off one of his coilguns.

The Nulljaw swallowed a second shard. Lok hadn't managed to prevent that. But he could stop a third. As the Nulljaw heated the projectile, Lok unleashed a cluster of missiles towards the shards around them before expanding the ashfield.

The Nulljaw vomited out another molten shard. The projectile burst into a shower of ash meters away from the ring. His ship was safe for the moment. But the Nulljaw was also safe from the ring weapons while the ashfield was up.

Lok still had four rockets out, even battered as they were. He set them after the Nulljaw like hunting hounds.

The monster retreated about a kilometer, at which point Lok gunned his engines to follow, so he could keep the H11s in radio range.

The Nulljaw spun, reverse thrusting to stop. Lok matched the move.

They faced each other

The Nulljaw turned and jetted away, towards the oncoming Shardstorm.

"Malvit," Lok swore. "It knows we'll follow."

"Then maybe we shouldn't," Faldos said.

"Can't. If we lose 'im now, the storm could carry it anywhere along the Shroud."

"Can your ashfield take that much matter coming at it at once?"

"Time to find out."

"Stars."

"Look, kid, this is where things are really gonna get shaky. I can't guarantee what'll happen next. If you want out, take one of the rockets now."

Faldos looked like he'd trade all the stars in the sky to be anywhere else. And yet he looked to Lok. "Just one question: Would my dad have turned back?"

Lok smiled. "Not in a thousand years."

Maybe that was the wrong thing to say, but it was true.

Faldos nodded like he expected as much. "I'm staying. We still have a monster to slay."

"Attaboy."

Lok increased thrust, chasing the Nulljaw. He directed the rockets to break off, fly to the edge of the debris field, then cut thrust and await further instructions. He didn't think they'd make it through the Shardstorm and he might need them later.

As Lok pivoted to follow the Nulljaw towards the oncoming shardstorm, the body of Scarlet Morn became clearer, the coloring of the dust now more of a blood-red shade, its star, smaller but brighter just creeping over its shoulder. Lok didn't like hunting this close to civilization.

Yet the position did offer one opportunity. He shuffled the thought away.

They were almost upon the storm. The Nulljaw hit the black wall like a meteor, sending out a craterous ripple that was quickly swallowed by the mass.

But Lok wasn't just gonna take the hit front-on. Moments before they struck the wave, Lok fired the magnetic pulser, and a cone of shards blew inward just ahead of them.

"Like dropping an anvil," Lok said.

"Huh?" Faldos blinked.

"You need to...never mind. Just buckle up."

Lok punched the throttle and the *Hunt or Be Hunted II* plunged into the Shardstorm.

# 13

# SHARDSTORM

---

ENTERING THE SHARDSTORM was the death of visibility. Shards bigger than Lok's ship churned in a gradient flow all the way down to specs measured in the microscopic.

And anything that might have been seen through that maelstrom was dashed by flares of ashmotes creating a barrier of burning debris around the *Hunt or Be Hunted II*.

Now and then a chunk worn down to the size of a fist might ding against the hull before completing its transformation into ash. Smaller shards were manageable. But…

One twice as big as the vessel materialized out of the gloom. Lok threw his throttle to the left. The edge of the massive shard skimmed over the ashfield. Only the first few meters of it could be ashed before it knocked one of the rotary guns off the satellite ring.

"That was a close one, huh, kid?" Lok said.

Faldos turned a nauseous color.

What seemed like another passing shard jerked towards them and spat a molten sphere from its mouth. Colliding dead on with the ashfield, the ball fizzled into ash uncomfortably close to the bridge.

The Nulljaw disappeared back into the black.

Lok lashed out with the magnetic pulser upon the storm like a machete through a jungle thicket. But the Nulljaw was not revealed. The pulser would eventually overheat, and it wasn't strong enough for the bigger shards, but Lok did buy some breathing room.

And so he caught his breath.

This time he spotted the Nulljaw breaking from its stealth near the ship's stern. Before he could unfold an illsur blade, It vomited an even larger molten projectile. Again, the ball disintegrated.

Lok swore the Nulljaw actually looked frustrated. He swung a blade from the ring but the Nulljaw pulled back into the storm's flow. For the moment, neither seemed able to hurt the other.

Lok wondered if he should've stocked ashquarrels, slow enough to be fired from within an ashfield. No, they'd just annoy the beast.

A chance shot with the pulser, stripped the Nulljaw of its camouflage.

The monster cruised alongside the *Hunt or Be Hunted II*. It fired nothing from its mouth, instead carrying in its clutchers a pair of shards each about the size of Lok. It tossed the first shard hard at the ship. The ashfield engaged and burned it away quickly. The Nulljaw tossed the second, this time with a good deal less force. The shard, moving slowly, passed through the ashfield, knocking against the hull. It damaged nothing but the paint job, which was already a lost cause.

Didn't matter, because the situation had just shifted.

"You're a smart one aren't ya?" Lok said.

Faldos swallowed hard. "It figured out how the ashfield works?"

"Seems that way."

Lok extended both illsur blades from their arms on the ring. The Nulljaw opened its mouth. Before they could clash a small mountain of a shard forced them to split up to evade. Lok lost sight of the monster.

More shots with the pulser didn't reveal anything. Lok was forced to stop. It was close to overheating. He kept the illsur blades ready, mechanical arms extended.

Two, no, three, medium-sized shards drifted onto collision courses with Lok's ship. Too slow for the ashfield. He sliced them to bits and let the remains burn up in the ashfield.

A fourth shard, the size of a landing shuttle, came from the flank and struck one of the blade arms. Only as it kept going down, pinning the arm to the ring, did Lok see that the Nulljaw was behind the shard.

It held the shard in two of its clutchers. Its third clutcher slithered out, reached around the shard and grabbed onto the blade arm. The metal strained. The other blade couldn't reach that far. Lok could only watch.

The metal arm snapped apart, the blade going with it. The beast pushed the shard lower, trying to break the entire satellite ring.

Lok momentarily pulled in the ashfield so he could get a shot off with his one working coilgun.

The Nulljaw took a cracked plate just above its dorsal thruster, and it retreated. But Lok knew he hadn't gotten the better of that trade. He expanded the ashfield again.

The Nulljaw made him wait before attacking again. Faldos looked so tense Lok wondered if he might crumple in on himself like a poorly made spring-toy.

"Kid, would you do me a favor and get to the engine room?"

"What? You mean it's time?"

"Yeah. Any minute now, I figure."

"All right. But I want you to know…I still think this is a terrible idea."

"Of course, it is. Now git!"

The Merrow boy scampered off the bridge, fingers tapping away at his controller.

The storm was starting to wane. Massive shards still flew around them, but fewer. Now when Lok fired the magnetic pulser, the faint outline of Scarlet Morn would come into view again.

The worst was still ahead. A shard easily five times the size of the *Hunt or Be Hunted II* flew at him. No way the pulser would even slow that. Lok went into evasive maneuvers.

The Nulljaw pounced. It carried a shard as before, but this time it simply chucked the chunk at Lok's ship. It went too fast, cracking and disintegrating on contact with the ashfield. But this cover of ash was what the Nulljaw wanted, coming in slower just behind it. It bit down squarely onto the remaining mechanical arm, ripping it clean off. At the same time, its three clutchers reached out, prying the one working coilgun off the ring. But it still wasn't done. It dove past the ring to smash nose-first into the hull.

The impact rattled the ship.

The Nulljaw flared its thrust, driving the entire ship towards the massive impending shard.

Lok grinned. This was like something he would pull.

No time to get out of the way of the gargantuan shard, so he did the opposite, and thrust towards it. He pulled the ring laterally along his ship, and just slammed the whole structure into the Nulljaw, knocking it off his hull.

In the last moment before impact, Lok rotated his ship, putting its stern towards the shard and hit the thrusters. The ashfield flared blinding ash-orange, struggling to burn away the too-massive projectile entering its domain. Alarms blared that the ashfield projector was near to burning out.

Impact. The whole ship jolted. But Lok's reverse thrust had slowed things enough. The damage was superficial. Just a few auxiliary thrusters crumpled and some minor hull damage.

But the shard still pushed them onward, towards the waiting Nulljaw. Its maw was open and ready to accept his ship.

However, the beast was also offering itself up on a platter.

Lok primed the Ashcannon. In turn, the Nulljaw ate a passing shard and spewed another molten projectile.

Either this beast was an idiot or a genius. Whether it'd planned this out or had just wanted to give Lok another obstacle, it didn't really matter. Lok needed to turn off his ashfield to fire the Ashcannon. If he wanted to take a shot at the Nulljaw, he'd have to allow the molten ball to strike true. An impossible choice and mere seconds to make it.

If that were his only choice.

Lok threw his throttle forward all the way. It'd take a moment to get up to speed, and the Nulljaw would never let him slip past. That was under normal circumstances.

"Kid…punch it."

"Can't believe I'm doing this again…"

On the other side of the ship, Faldos' puppet Graves threw the quick release lever they'd installed earlier, dropping the *Hunt or Be Hunted II*'s core into its fuel reservoir.

The ship shot forward with blinding speed. Lok pressed back in his seat in spite of the inertial dampeners.

The molten ball turned into a smear of ash and beyond the Nulljaw waited with open maw. It probably thought it'd won. It thought it'd understood how his ashfield worked. If it wasn't moving then it should've been safe.

But speed was relative.

The moment before impact, Lok smiled. "You lose, idiot."

Glowing orange motes of ash cascaded around the Nulljaw as the two bodies collided. A tremor carried across the starship, jarring Lok's very bones.

The viewport was filled with blinding orange light from the ashfield battling to atomize so much kuron metal.

At long last it cleared.

The entire outer layer of the Nulljaw's armor had been stripped off its body. Only smaller scale-like needles remained among a now sinuous body removed of its bulk.

The Nulljaw writhed in agony, a sparse scattering of ashmotes still working at it in places. It opened its jagged maw in a silent scream of radiant orange dust.

"You see that kid?" Lok laughed.

"I…do." Faldos said over the radio. "It…looks like it's also still alive."

"Yep. But ashes, finally giving that thing a real hit feels good, don't it? And let's see him shrug off my toys without all that thick armor."

"Lok, I think you're forgetting something."

"What's that?"

"Just the little fact that WE JUST BURNT OUT OUR ENGINE! We're dead in the water!"

"So plop in the spare core."

"How do you expect me to do that? I'm not a starship engineer!"

"It's easy, the spare is already there. Just flip the lever up to bring the core back up, then swap it out with the new one. If you get confused, there's a locker in that room. The third one on the left should be a book titled, 'Vosta's Guide on Engine Repair for Idiots Who Only Know How to Hunt.'"

The shardstorm was clearing out, larger chunks having gone past, and even the dust thinning. Lok checked his weapons. One in particular, the controls for the harpoon gun was offline. The turret must've been damaged during the fight. Probably the front-on impact with the beast.

"Why can't you do this?" Faldos asked.

"I got a date with a Nulljaw."

Lok threw his Twinshot over one shoulder, his blastspear over the other, and slipped his Kalclaw over his left arm. He popped open the hatch on the bridge, and got a good view of the Nulljaw without anything between them.

The monster turned it's eyeless gaze towards the *Hunt or Be Hunted II*. It bled ash, and radiated rage. Ice shot through Lok's veins, but he didn't shrink back. He would not falter under fear. He met that eyeless gaze, daring it to come after him.

True, his ship currently had no actual ashfield or any other real defenses.

But the Nulljaw didn't know that.

Slowly, the beast turned away, towards Scarlet Morn.

"That's what I thought." Lok leaped off the bridge, and sprinted across the top deck toward the bow of the ship.

The Nulljaw's tail was beginning to flare orange. It was getting ready to jet out of here, and they'd have no means of following. Unless…

Lok reached the bow, and threw hands onto the harpoon gun. The weapon, as long as he was tall, looked still in working order. Just the remote controls had failed.

And that's what manual was for. He pulled the final harpoon out of the nearby slot, already a cable hooked up. He slid it into the gun.

The Nulljaw started moving. Lok fired.

The Nulljaw either didn't notice or didn't care about the small metal spike flying towards it. Mistake.

The harpoon struck home, into the Nulljaw's wounded side, even further stripped of armor than before. The blade embedded, spraying its quick-setting cement and anchoring the cable to the beast. Lok braced himself on the gun and waited.

The cable went taut, and the entire ship lurched forward. The cable held and they went cruising through space, dragged by the Nulljaw. Lok very nearly lost his grip and went tumbling back down the deck.

"What was that!?" Faldos exclaimed.

"We're going along for a ride. Courtesy of the Nulljaw."

# 14

# TERMINAL VECTOR

FALDOS SAW BY red emergency lights. His hands shook as he struggled to remove bolts from the ship's core one by one. The tremble in his arms had nothing to do with the tool's vibration.

Needle-size shards peppered the other side of the hull like bullets.

Faldos struggled to get a bolt off.

He hung from a cable, tossed over one of the tree ship's branches, affording him a better position to remove the core. The cable started in a metal hand gripping the back of his suit and ended in Graves' outstretched arm. Trying not to feel like a condemned man to be hung, he flicked a fully loosened nut off and moved to the next.

The rain clatter of shards grew louder.

Abruptly he felt the weight of his body in his suit relieve somewhat and the branch bearing the cable rose higher. Artificial gravity was beginning to fail. And with it, inertial dampening.

A heavy impact sent him swinging on his cable. When his trajectory swung him back he barely grabbed hold of the core's housing.

Cursing, he chanced a look at his controller's screen, displaying the ship's external cameras.

The Nulljaw was dragging them through the edge of the Shroud, against any large shards it passed. Lok dove into a hatch before another impact scattered shards across the surface of the ship. Ready this time, Faldos weathered the tremors.

Back inside the ship, Lok fired off a plethora of missiles, some exploded against shards, destroying or knocking them away. Others, the front-burning blazerunners, seared the Nulljaw's thinned flesh, ushering it, like cattle prods. He gave it no chance to turn around and break free of its unwanted tow.

As Lok brought to bear the rest of the weapons he could still fire without a core, Faldos turned his attention back to his own task. He cranked off the last bolt, the impact driver struggling with the final one. But after it came loose he barely kicked himself out of the way before the core rolled out of the housing. A twitch reflex of his hands let him catch the burned out core with Graves. But to move forward, the cable had pulled with him, dragging Faldos up to slam into the tree branch he was draped over.

He then tried to lower himself but found the cable was caught.

Gravity is lower, it'll be fine he reasoned, and then released himself.

Faldos hit the floor with an audible smack and considerably more pain than he'd expected.

Lok ran into the engineering room then. He immediately stopped and looked down at Faldos splayed across the deck.

"Good job." Lok offered a hand and hauled Faldos' to his feet.

"Whatever I'm being paid," Faldos said. "I think I want a raise." He had Graves toss the spent core aside.

"I don't think you'll be disappointed."

Faldos looked back at the open manual and read aloud.

"'Reminder: don't be an idiot and forget to open the safety catch on the new core before installation. Reach inside that hand-sized hole—don't worry it doesn't bite—feel for a lever and pull it. Not too hard, don't break it ya meathead.' Lok, who wrote this?"

"Live long enough and you'll meet her. Keep on, I've got a Nulljaw to fry."

The Logra turned his eyes back on his cuffcomp from which he was commanding the ship's weapons.

*Live long enough...* Not for the first time Faldos wondered if he should've taken his early out on this suicide mission.

Faldos pulled the safety latch on the fresh core, and, with Graves, hoisted the whole thing into the housing.

Faldos drew himself back up by means of the cable and started screwing in nuts. He had even more trouble getting the impact driver lined up more than once from all the bumping and jostling, the ever present reminder of impending doom.

But the real fear came when it all stopped.

"What happened?" He asked.

"We're fully clear of the Shroud." Lok said. "In open space again."

"That's...good, right?"

"Yeah...except that I'm out of bullets and missiles. And I think our quarry is figuring that out." Lok studied his cuff. "It wants to cut the line but it's already lost a lot of teeth and I've charged the cable with ash. Just barely enough juice for that. He's looking at us now."

Faldos could easily pull up the feed himself. But with his shaking arms it was all he could do to not drop the impact. He leaned away from the core, trying to shake it off.

*Come on, coward, you've almost died before. You should be used to it.*

"It's getting closer now." Lok said, oblivious. "I think he's ready to risk another pass at us. I'm gonna launch some more of the H11s. But don't got many to spare for the last resort. Which we're getting a lot closer to." Despite the words Lok was the picture of cool.

Of course, this was routine for him. Faldos could ask the old hunter to finish the job but to admit defeat at this, the one task he'd been trusted with...

Faldos pulled one of his suit gloves off, even as the hand shook. Then he bit down on his thumb, hard. Just when the pain told him it was too far, he bit a little harder then released. He tugged the glove back over the reddened flesh. It felt stupid and childish, but less so than being too scared to thread down a nut.

"Problem there, kid?"

"Nothing. I got it."

He screwed down the rest of the bolts without so much as a tremble. Consulting the book, he found he'd neared the end of the section.

Faldos read aloud, at first a whisper but getting louder as he went.

"Congratulations, you've just performed the most basic actions of starship repair. To start up your new core, pump the primer lever five times, then throw the power switch up and…pour a cup of tea and sit back for the ten minutes it'll take to warm up! Who said anything about a ten minute wait!?

"Just do it!"

Faldos did, falling back on muttering some of the milder curses he'd learned since becoming a spacer.

"Done!" he finally cried out.

"Almost." Lok unhooked a black cylinder from his belt and tossed it to Faldos. He barely caught it.

"Press that to the side of the core and twist," Lok said

Faldos did and the cylinder stuck in place as firmly as if it's been welded.

"What is it?" he asked.

"Insurance," was Lok's only explanation.

Faldos lowered himself to the floor. He unhooked the puppet's hand from his suit and retracted it.

Lok peered down at his cuffcomp, expression lost in the darkness of his fur. But something subtle in his stance grew firm.

"You may want to hold onto—"

Then impact. It shook the *Hunt or Be Hunted II* so strongly Faldos nearly fell over. Metal screamed out in a too-familiar sound.

Lok sighed. "Faldos…"

"I know. It's chewing on the hull."

Lok only nodded and shrugged the Twinshot into his grip. "Kid, I think maybe you should have taken that rocket when you had the chance."

A panicked laugh escaped his lips. "Too late now?"

"You fly away in a rocket now, you won't make it thirty meters. We make our stand here."

Faldos planted Graves right in front of him. Then considered, and moved himself further back, hiding behind a wide root of the ship's tree.

Another metal scream rang out. Then came the raspy sliding of something entering the ship.

Lok glanced at his cuff. "That'll be the first clutcher."

"Sh-shouldn't we close this compartment's hatch?" Faldos asked, hating how his voice cracked.

"It'd get through either way. I don't want it flying at us when it blows off."

Faldos only nodded, not trusting his own voice. He held his controller in a vice-grip, the trembling threatened to start again. Instead of taking a glove off he bit the inside of his cheek. The shakes were delayed.

Lok tapped his cuff, activating his onboard countermeasures.

The first of the autoguns started firing, echoing down the corridor. Neither of them spoke, but a mutual glance was exchanged. The gunfire abruptly cut off, replaced by the sound of the gun being smashed.

More metal sliding. It hastened, the clutcher launching at something. Hiss of acid on metal, then something thrashed wildly.

There was a small tugging at Lok's cheeks. "It found the Deathgaze corpse."

A second sound of sliding metal. A second clutcher.

Soon the second autogun fired, bullets ricocheting off the bulkhead. It too was silenced. A slight hissing noise. A leaky air compressor. The sliding rasp drew towards this other sound. There was a clanking and banging of the clutcher entering the workshop. Lok sighed but tapped his cuff again.

The slew of mines on the walls activated and every powertool, bolt and scrap of metal became shrapnel in the resulting explosion. Lok closed his eyes, pained. Faldos didn't blame him.

The third autogun fired. They could see the muzzle flare with their own eyes down the dim hall.

The gunfire rang out for a few more seconds before it was silenced in a crunch of metal.

The sliding and scraping was close now and something dark was visible.

Lok aimed the Twinshot down the hatch. He ran a finger over the first trigger, then the second.

Faldos raised all six of Graves' arms. His own arms were fully shaking and a little pain wasn't making it go away. Cursing under his breath didn't help much either.

"Lok?" he finally said.

"Yeah, kid?"

"Are we gonna die?"

"That's not the question you should be asking. You should be asking if we can kill this monster? Because that's the only way we live. So, I'm going to ask you, can you hunt this monster with me?"

"I...yeah."

"Say it."

"I can hunt this monster with you."

"Loud enough for the Nulljaw to hear."

"I can hunt this monster with you!"

And remarkably he was starting to believe it.

He wasn't here to survive. He was here to slay.

The shakes subsided, and he was able to hold his controller with a sure grip. Other thoughts faded. It was just him, Lok, the puppet and the thing coming down the hall.

A shadowy flicker was all they saw before the clutcher speared into the engine room. Thrashing against every surface, it sent tools flying at dangerous speeds.

It was shaped like a great, eyeless, black serpent, almost as wide around as Lok was tall. Most of its armor had been stripped by the ashfield attack, but it still bore enough scales to protect it from the most measly weapons of vermin.

Faldos shrank back and fired Graves' gun. He missed and put a bullet in the bulkhead.

Lok fired his first barrel.

There was a blinding flash and a deafening bang. The slug ripped through the clutcher, tearing a torso-sized hole out the back of it. Black armor and flesh hit the bulkhead. The clutcher twisted in pain, then sprang at the source of its attack.

Lok dove, the clutcher brushing his scuff fur as it passed above him. As the teeth bit down into the floor, he slashed an ashen claw into it's flank. He leaped aside as the clutcher made another lunge. The old hunter was a machine.

Well, Faldos had a machine too. He took more careful aim with Graves' Vacgore gun, waiting for a clear shot.

At the same time Lok rolled up to his feet, raised the Twinshot again.

But the clutcher coiled, like a spring then sprang with unexpected speed. It crashed into both the hunter and the puppet.

Lok's feet left the floor and he pounded into the bulkhead beside.

Graves was flung into the tree branches above. Shards of wood rained down on Faldos. Then the puppet landed in a crash beside him.

But the clutcher seemed to be pained by its own attack. The front portion of its sinuous body, past where Lok put a hole in it, was moving stiffly. Lok had hurt it for sure.

Lok jumped up, but immediately had to duck to keep from getting brained by a flying impact driver.

"Faldos! The puppet, hold it down. I need one more clean shot!"

"O-on it!" He fumbled with the controller and drove the puppet onto its feet. Graves sprang onto the clutcher, six handed vice-grip holding it in place.

The clutcher kept whipping around the room, but now with a puppet dangling from it.

"Find something to grab onto!" Lok ordered.

Graves released two of its hands to scrape at the floor, but found no purchase. He switched to Graves' main thruster. The puppet rocketed up to the ceiling, bringing the clutcher with it. The clutcher pushed back, dragging them both along the ceiling until Graves managed to grab hold of a thick branch, grown along the bulkhead. Faldos then anchored both of the puppet's feet into the ceiling. The clutcher, finally, was brought to rein.

"That'll do, kid!"

Lok rushed over, bounded up and thrust the Twinshot up into the clutcher's armor, perpendicular to the spot where he'd shot it. He pulled the trigger. The resulting blast made a crater in the clutcher's flesh. It let out one last throw of pain, before the front half of the clutcher ripped off completely.

The half of the clutcher that remained trembled in pain before dragging back out the way it came, vanishing into the gloom of the emergency lights.

"We did it?" Faldos gaped. "We did it! Ha! Take that!"

"We got *one* of them."

There was more scraping down the hall coming closer. Faldos swallowed.

More tremors rang out. Lok checked his cuff and cursed.

"The Beast is wrecking my ship." He shouldered the empty Twinshot and drew his blastspear. In his other hand he drew a particle pistol. Faldos anchored Graves again and readied the Vacgore gun once more.

"I know you're new to this," Lok said, "but try aiming when you fire."

"That's easier said than done when a nightmare tongue is coming at you! Lot easier when it's not moving. You're welcome, by the way. For holding it down."

"Ya don't gotta take advice so personally. But…not bad, all things considered. Now let's focus."

Faldos nodded, but hesitated. "What is that smell?!"

"That'd be the clutcher. Stinks, doesn't it? Most of 'em do."

"Like a Sundering. How long was that anyway? It's gotta be ten minutes right?"

Lok checked his cuff. "That was a hair over four. Got about six more."

"No…"

"Yeah."

The clutchers were close now, slithering down the hall.

"You can go ahead and start shooting now," Lok said.

"Don't gotta tell me twice."

Graves' gun blasted at the clutchers, striking one of them with a satisfying thunk. Lok fired beams of blue at the same time, burning into the other.

"Hey, I actually hit something!" Faldos cheered.

"Like fish in a barrel. Keep going."

Faldos reloaded and fired again. Another shot landed home on the second one. Lok fired too, burning a scar along the other. It didn't slow the clutchers much. By the time he reloaded again, the clutchers were bursting through the port, stretching the metal to fit both. Faldos fired a third time, ripping a fist-sized hole into its upper 'jaw'. The clutcher lunged, smashing into Graves and trying to crush the puppet between its teeth. But those same teeth had been mangled by the Deathgaze's acid and struggled to crush the resilient Graves.

"Hope you like meals served hot," Faldos growled. The plasma torch erupted into the clutcher's maw. It bucked and shook, but Graves' metal grip held fast. He next fired up the buzzsaw, ashen blade cutting into one side of the clutcher's maw, while he fired the laser into the other side.

Lok fought a much cleaner battle by comparison. He jumped, ducked and wove around the second clutcher. This one had been in the workshop and bore the scars. Lok targeted its shrapnel wounds, blowing holes deeper into the beast's flesh. The clutcher roiled with pain.

Just as Faldos' hopes were rising, the clutcher chasing Lok moved laterally, catching the wire from Graves' back and wrenched the controller well out of Faldos' grip. The controller clattered back down to the floor, halfway across the room. Right in the middle of the carnage.

With the puppet now directionless, Faldos' clutcher finally knocked Graves loose. The puppet bounced when it hit the floor. Unhindered, the clutcher pulled searching for its next victim. Faldos prayed it would not be him.

It wasn't, though not much better. The clutcher responded to the building glow of the core, twisting with interest, as if at a sweet scent.

Faldos eyed his controller, so far from the tree root he'd found shelter behind. He thought of all the horrible ways he could die charging out there. He also thought of all the merciless killing the Nulljaw could do if it got that new core.

The clutcher moved. So did Faldos.

Sprinting across the room, bounding over the rolling dead core, sliding under the clutcher and nearly tripping on a wrench before he finally snatched up his precious controller.

The clutcher was less than a meter from the new core.

Faldos hand moved instinctively, thoughts ceding to action.

The explosive punch of the mini rocket knocked the clutcher off course, getting a mouthful of tree trunk instead. Graves then sprang onto the creature, anchoring its feet into its body and firing the Vacgore gun point blank. The beastly limb recoiled, all focus away from the core.

Faldos pumped his fist with triumph.

Unfortunately, he didn't notice the other clutcher springing towards him until it was too late. He stumbled seeing his death race forward.

Then he was sliding across the floor and Lok was where he'd stood a moment ago. The clutcher slammed home, crushing Lok against the side wall.

Faldos' heart skipped a beat. He might've thought of how this would end for him, how without Lok he would be doomed. But he didn't get that far. Instead his mind just kept playing the last sight of his father over and over. Here another man died and he was helpless to-

"Wipe the worry off her face, kid! G-got 'im...right where I want 'im!" It was a throaty, animal voice, but still clearly Lok's.

Rising, Faldos got a better look.

Lok was not in fact crushed to paste. He was instead somehow holding the massive writhing creature's maw open with his hands.

And…was he getting bigger?

•  •  •

SIX MONTHS HAD been a good streak.

Lok held open the clutcher's false mouth with rapidly expanding muscles. He held the upper jaw with his kalclaw and the lower with his bare hand. One tooth jutted up right through his naked palm. He didn't care. He wasn't feeling pain right now. His muscles had now swelled to double their usual size and were still growing. There came the unforgettable feeling of his bones rapidly thickening. But all of these details faded away, as did all emotions except that of a mono-focused predatory fury.

Lok hated going feral.

He dug the kalclaw into the flesh of the upper mouth, bladed fingers glowing with ashen energy. The clutcher pulled back and slammed him against the wall. Bones cracked, but were already reknitting. Going feral did have its perks.

Lok dove his claw deeper, the upper lip breaking apart as it turned to ash. He slammed the kalclaw down onto the bottom jaw, beginning to ash that too. The clutcher pulled back, trying to retreat as it realized its mistake. Lok dug his feet in, and with a pop that might've come from either of them, pulled the lower jaw off in a spray of ash and black bits. The clutcher coiled and slithered backwards.

*No, you don't get off that easily.*

Lok dashed after it, scooping up his fallen blastspear, pulling the trigger so the ashen spearhead extended, then tossed it like a javelin. It flew right down the clutcher's 'throat', piercing the flesh within. The clutcher floundered on its way out the doorway, and down the hall. By the time the blastspear finally fell out, a full meter of the clutcher's length had turned to ash. The wounded clutcher disappeared back into the gloom.

Lok grabbed his blastspear back up and whirled around, eager to find another opponent.

Faldos, by means of Graves, had managed to glue his clutcher's mouth shut, and was now torching it, burning it with a laser on one side, and slicing up the other with an ashen buzzsaw. And every few seconds he fired another Vacgore bullet down into the creature. The damage was starting to add up, chunks of armored flesh falling away. The clutcher in reply was thrashing, knocking the puppet from floor to ceiling, but that hadn't seemed to have done much. Graves really was sturdy.

Lok ended the stalemate by plunging the blastspear down into the clutcher, nailing it to the floor. But the clutcher twisted, ripping its flesh free of the blade, only a gouge of its meat missing. The clutcher shook off the puppet and pulled back down the hall, abandoning the fight.

"I h-had that one," Faldos said.

"Uh-huh," Lok said pacing.

He actually grinned then. "But I'm glad you're alive." Faldos looked him up and down. "What happened to you?"

"Gone feral," he growled.

"Does it hurt?"

"It will. Later." He retrieved his weapons and slid them back onto his person.

The lights shifted from emergency red back to full brightness.

"Power's back!" Faldos said.

A metallic screech echoed down the hall. Lok crouched, listening with ears sharper than ever.

The ashing Nulljaw was eating its way into his ship. Once he remembered he had a cuffcomp, he confirmed with the horrifying image of the beast chewing its way into his hull. The battle with the clutchers had been won, but they were about to lose the war.

No.

Not again. Not this ship.

Lok dropped down on all fours and ran.

"Where are you going!?" Faldos cried.

Lok tried to reply but it only came out as a snarl. He bounded down the scarred and scraped corridors of his home. It wasn't long before he saw it. The hall ended abruptly, splitting into empty space. Just beyond, was a wretched body of broken kuron plates and foul night flesh. The Nulljaw was digging its way through the *Hunt or Be Hunted II*, nearly piercing the Ashcannon barrel.

Lok sprang out of the mouth of the broken corridor, and laid his claws on the Nulljaw. He scampered across its flesh, searching. Hunting. He found it: the weak spot. Within the scar torn by K'val, and down to the even deeper gouge left by Graves. Into this spot, Lok drove his ashen kalclaw. Kuron and flesh splintered away into motes of ash. He ripped it out and hit it again. Deeper, until his elbow was scraping kuron armor. But the mass of flesh was resisting the ash. Too much of it to burn away at once. Lok cursed, but he had other weapons. He ripped the claw free, pointed his particle pistol down the hole and fired. The blue beam bored like a drill. Lok emptied the weapon, tossed it aside, then drove the blastspear down the even deeper hole. He pulled the trigger.

The Nulljaw actually twisted in pain, stalling in its demolition of the starship.

"Hurt my ship? Destroy my home!? Ya think ya can get the better of *me*?" Lok's words were barely more than a growl.

Lok couldn't thrust the spear any deeper, so he tore it out and started ripping up the sides of the hole. He only had the kalclaw on one hand, using his natural claws on the other. He barely noticed when the nails broke off and his hand grew bloody. Who cared that his initial burst of feral healing was over?

"You're the prey, not me," he growled, both hands ripping away armor and flesh.

Something landed beside him and he whirled, almost putting a claw into Graves. His brain took a moment to catch up, and he traced the puppet's cable back to Faldos, standing in the broken corridor. With quaking knees, but he was standing.

The kid opened his mouth to speak and due to the vacuum between them, his words started quiet over the radio.

"Lok, respectfully...this isn't the plan, you suicidal maniac!"

"Ash the plan!" he growled back.

"Even you can't kill this thing with your bare hands!"

"I sure can try!"

A fire lit in the kid's eyes and Graves crouched, ready to pounce.

"Then you'll have to tear through Graves first! I'm not gonna let you get yourself killed after you went to all the trouble of saving me!"

"You're not a hunter, Faldos—"

"-But I'm here, aren't I?"

The kid's knees quaked again. But he stood his ground, meeting Lok eye to eye while a living weapon meters away ravaged the ship.

*But I'm here aren't I?*

Lok had heard words so very similar before. When he'd been less experienced and a kind of stupid that had nothing to do with going feral. He'd tried to take on a Murdra Hive Queen holed up beneath a newly constructed colony. He'd come alone, been surrounded, and his hunting career had looked to be at an abrupt end.

And yet one of the Merrow engineers hadn't fled from the beast like the rest. He jumped down into the fray and convinced Lok to pull back so they could trap the hive in the architectural skeleton of the new colony.

Lok had objected then too.

*I don't need your help, you aren't a hunter.*

*But I am here.*

He looked down at his hands, covered in black gore. A crater of flesh below him, but still nowhere near the core or other vitals.

It'd been a long time since Lok had had someone to tell him when to pull back. And he'd called Sendro the fool.

Lok forced his mouth to form cohesive words.

"You're right, Faldos."

"Wait, really?" Faldos asked.

Lok nodded. "To the bridge."

Faldos nodded back. He offered a hand, through Graves. Lok took it, and they boosted off the Nulljaw, back into what was left of his ship. They ran.

"Kid, I still got feral fog," Lok said. "Remind me what the plan is from here."

"Depends. Are we to the final push yet? Do we have any rockets left?"

It took Lok a moment to determine that answer himself.

"Uh, two…but I need to save those until the end. Why aren't there more? There should be more." Was it time to launch the last two? Were they there yet? No. "There's one other thing we can still try first."

He sprinted down the hall on all fours again, dashing up a ladder and down another hall into the bridge. The whole trip in less than ten seconds. What he saw out of the viewport turned his heart to ash. The ship was ruptured around the Nulljaw, its body now deep inside. Cable spilled out of the wound like blood from veins.

Lok threw the throttle forward. He turned the helm one way… then back the other, when he remembered he needed to leave the field. The Nulljaw shifted, sensing the movement. But it didn't stop. It dove deeper.

Scarlet Morn grew clear ahead, its red body dominating the scene. Even the thin metal ring of Ruby Roost was visible now. Lok saw the tails of distant rockets cresting the edge of the Shroud. He finally remembered the four H11s he'd left behind. They were back within radio signal. Lok still had tools left.

He couldn't, no- wouldn't, fight this beast like a beast.

He'd hunt it like a man.

He swung the rockets around towards the Nulljaw, activating their ashfields. A warning chime from the ship signaled that artificial-gravity was failing. Lok didn't care. The first rocket plunged into the beast's back. The ashfield flared, getting half its length into the beast before it shorted out. He buried another in its flank.

The Nulljaw ripped itself free of the ship, spraying shards of metal everywhere, orange mist flaring from its mouth and the new hole in its back.

"Hope that hurts," Lok said, sending in the next two rockets.

The Nulljaw cast out its clutchers, what was left of them, and dislodged the two H11s in its body, then knocked two approaching ones off path. The Nulljaw thrust away from the ship as the rockets pulled around for another pass. It used its clutchers to block the next approach, ashfields burning through them, but giving the Nulljaw an opening to bite down on the rockets, crushing two of them in its maw.

The Nulljaw spat the rocket slag, tearing through the other two rockets.

The Nulljaw paused; perhaps it was getting the better of it, or perhaps hesitating. Lok didn't. He swung the ship around, priming the Ashcannon.

Faldos finally made it into the room. "What's happening?"

"I'm ending this."

The Nulljaw turned to flee. It didn't matter. It wouldn't get far.

Lok pulled the trigger.

# 15

# ORBITAL PREY

---

**THE ASHCANNON EXPLODED.** Well, it didn't explode, per se. The sliding armature struck a warped rail at speed and ripped its internals apart. Metal shards sprayed out the hole in the side of the ship. A spinning projectile did fly out of the front of the gun, but at less than a quarter the speed, and the shock of the crash had thrown the aim off. It completely missed the Nulljaw.

"Malvit!" Lok slammed a fist into a console. "Malvit, malvit, malvit!" The console was completely crushed when he was done with it. Lok hoped that hadn't been important.

Both were quiet for a moment.

"The backup plan?" Faldos said.

"...seems like it's come to that."

"But you said that was a really bad idea."

"It is. Let's go." Lok punched the throttle, driving the ship as fast as it'd go. Warnings flared up, chimes ringing out. *The Hunt or Be Hunted II* was in bad shape. But repairs would have to wait. All that mattered right now was his prey: The Nulljaw.

The monster fled towards easier targets. Its burning tail was getting faint. It needed a new core and fast. It raced towards a group of mining ships making for Ruby Roost's docks.

Lok left the controls. He didn't need to be here to travel in a straight line.

"Where are you going?" Faldos asked.

"To the bow. I've gotta get the harpoon gun. Take Graves, to get the spare in the armory. You'll need him to carry it to…uh…the rocket deck! There's two I kept in reserve for us. Ashing feral brain."

"Anything else?"

"I think…harpoons! More harpoons! And cables! Ashing feral brain. And seal up your suit."

"My suit has been since this started, but why?"

The ship chimed out that the breathability barrier was failing. Lok had felt the air pressure changing before the alert had even gone out.

"That's why."

Lok almost forgot to tap on his personal breath barrier, before he cracked the top hatch. Lok drifted up, and shot his kalclaw's grappling hook into the hull. Slamming the retractor, Lok slingshot himself to the front of the ship.

He slid to a stop in front of the harpoon gun. How did this thing come off again…? He didn't even have an ashing wrench. He had to stop himself from trying to rip the whole thing off with his hands.

The cuffcomp! There was a remote release in case he needed to cut off the line. Lok tapped his cuff a few seconds, struggling with his sized-up fingers before he finally got it to comply with his request. The harpoon gun unhooked but remained still. He recalled that the turret had been damaged.

Lok gave it a sharp tug, and the whole thing finally came free. He was going to run to the nearest hatch, but decided it would be faster to simply grapple down into the hole the Nulljaw had made. From there, it was a kick down a hall into the rocket deck. Here the two remaining rockets waited.

After what felt like an hour to his impatient mind, but was probably only a couple minutes, Faldos arrived, Graves with the second harpoon gun and more ammo. Lok once again struggled to remember how to perform a basic task.

The console! He could do it from his cuffcomp, but the console was easier. He tapped away, opening both rockets' cargo compartments. He hauled his harpoon launcher inside, and Faldos did the same with the other.

Lok nodded with approval. "Now weld both of them in place. Sturdy as you can get them, they're gonna take a lot of weight."

Faldos got to work with Graves, first reloading the weapons, then welding them.

Lok stared at the two rockets.

"What is it?" Faldos asked.

"Just…trying to figure out how this will work. There aren't any turrets in the rockets. I can't remote control them."

"You're saying they need to be fired manually?"

"Yeah…" He looked down at Faldos. He couldn't ask him to—

"Not a problem," the boy said quickly.

Lok blinked.

"It's not?"

"No. We're out of the Shroud. There's no interference. I can control Graves by radio."

"Kid, you're a genius. Or I'm an idiot. Feral brain." Lok tapped at the console. "All right, it's all set. I've managed to link the controls to your cuffcomp. Once the puppet and I are in the rockets, launch us both. Put them at full burn. No point in leaving anything in reserve now."

"Okay but…are you sure this is a good idea?"

"Only one I got."

Faldos studied him, then nodded. "Good hunting."

"Thanks. See you in a minute."

Lok stepped inside the rocket, and closed the hatch. The rockets dropped out of their tubes into space. He braced himself to the padded back. He was about to go very fast in a very short amount of time, with no inertial dampeners to soften it.

He waited. What was taking the boy so long? All he had to do was press one—

Lok flattened against the back of the rocket as it took off. He was stuck like that for a few minutes before the acceleration leveled off and he could finally lean forward.

He checked his cuff for the rocket's front camera.

The Nulljaw was almost to one of the mining vessels. A big wedge with only drilling tools on its satellite ring. No real means of defense. If reached, the beast would make short work of it. Lok thought he could see panicking miners on the top deck, fleeing to the nearest port. Lok wouldn't allow that. He opened the compartment.

They were coming up parallel with the Nulljaw, a couple hundred meters between them at most. The beast opened its mouth, bearing jagged, ash-eaten teeth at the mining ship.

Lok put his harpoon into its lower chin. Faldos, through Graves, fired his own, taking the beast in the side. As one they turned their rockets away from the vulnerable ship. The lines went taut, cables trembling at the tremendous amounts of mass they were pulling.

The Nulljaw's teeth closing down on nothing but void as it was dragged away from the mining ship. The beast roiled, turning its fiery tail in the opposite direction of the rockets' pull.

For a breath-stealing moment, they hung in a battle of thrust. But slowly, so much so that Lok barely believed, they began to crawl, meter by meter towards the red planet below.

The Nulljaw thrashed and bit, but it failed to reach the cables dragging it. The stumps of its clutchers were too short to do anything of use.

Lok grinned. "A monster like you was born and bred in the void. Wonder just how well you'd do on a planet with real gravity? I reckon you wouldn't like it one bit. Lemme introduce a feeling that must be real alien to you: falling."

The Nulljaw writhed with greater fervor, trying all its might to buck the needles piercing its mighty flesh. But it was tired, weak, wounded.

And it was staring death in the face.

They were starting to work their way past Ruby Roost now. The station was too close for comfort but still out of reach from the monster.

Shocked faces looked out of viewports at the scene. The feral part of Lok's brain reveled at this. At the cattle seeing just what predators that the hounds protected them from. He pounded this thought into submission. He was not better than them. He would not let himself think like a monster. He hunted monsters.

Without warning, the Nulljaw jetted laterally, towards the station. It had more juice left than he'd expected. Lok cursed and shifted the rocket to adjust, but he was too late. It dug its teeth into the station's hull.

Lok's mind raced. Not only was the station in danger, but the Nulljaw had anchored itself, enough to hold back the rockets' thrusts. It refused to slacken its grip on the station. Like a springhound with a chew toy. He checked the fuel on the rockets. They were made for long distances, but their fuel would only go so far. They'd already used a lot just dragging the Nulljaw off course.

"Pardon, kid," Lok said. "But I gotta take another swing at the beast."

"What? Again?"

"This time I don't gotta a choice."

"You know, I'm not there to pull you out again."

"Trust me, I wish I wasn't, either."

Lok jumped out of the rocket. He snagged the harpoon cable with his kalclaw's cable ascender and rappelled down towards the Nulljaw, passing uncomfortably close to the rocket's exhaust.

He landed in a crouch on the black plates of the Nulljaw's lower chin. He pulled his kalclaw back and drove it deep between the plates. The claw flared with ashen energy.

But the ash worked too slow. Even thin and shredded, pure kuron was still pure kuron. Frustrated, he pulled the claw back and jabbed it down again and again, bits of kuron, too small, were torn up in the process. He growled at the beast that refused to die.

The Nulljaw didn't care. Lok may as well have been trying to push a moon off its orbit. Beating his chest with one arm, he pulled back and brought himself to reign. He couldn't afford to lose control again.

*Don't be Sendro. Think.*

He knew there was a solution here, but his feral mind was too dumb to see it. He couldn't attack the teeth themselves, they were even thicker than the armor on the chin.

He needed…needed…

Patience.

Lok took a breath. He sat back on the body of the monster, and waited. Waited for the answer to come to him. His mind was weak, but his memory held experience.

Kuron plates. Too dense to break, even with ash-wrought hands. No bombs or missiles to blast his way through. No way to break the hold…

…unless…

He looked up, to where the Nulljaw's teeth pierced the station's outer hull. The metal was warped and straining, but holding for the moment. Lok couldn't tell immediately what alloy it was. But he could tell it wasn't pure kuron or illsur. Which meant that it'd probably ash pretty easily.

Lok barreled forward and pounced across the gap. He landed kalclaw-first, driving it deep into the metal punctured by the monster's lower teeth. He felt the alloy fragment into ash.

With a savage howl, Lok dashed forward, ripping the station's skin apart.

Like rotting skin on a corpse, the metal came apart and the Nulljaw's lower teeth broke free of the hull. Its upper teeth held on for just a moment, before the strain on that part of the hull finally broke it off too.

The Nulljaw tumbled away from the station, mouth gaping silently. Lok wished it'd roar in impotent defiance. That it'd let out a cry of anguish, knowing that it'd been beaten by Lok Brightslayer.

But that, of course, was impossible in space.

Lok finally allowed his shoulders to slump. He exhaled.

The Nulljaw had left several teeth in the hull. Leaning down, Lok ripped one out and stuffed the trophy into his belt. He'd return for the rest later.

"All right, kid, bring the ship around. I wanna watch the rest of the show from my own chair."

"You...do remember I don't know how to pilot a ship, right?"

Lok bit down a retort that he would've regretted. Instead he took a deep breath and used his cuff to instruct the ship to meet him along the station's ring. Patiently.

As it approached, the ship looked even worse than it had before. The Nulljaw had gotten close to eating halfway through it. But it was over now. He could spend the reward money fixing up his starship.

The ship cruised in close and slowed enough that Lok could use his kalclaw to grapple up to what was left of the satellite ring, then swing down to the hull. He climbed into the bridge, Faldos' eyes glued to the screen on his controller.

Lok was far more interested in the natural sight of the front viewport.

The rockets were taking the Nulljaw down, down, down towards the planet below.

It was slow going, the Nulljaw keeping its own tail flaring, but the progress was steady. The rockets should have just enough fuel. It was over. They needed only wait before gravity finally took-

"Lok!" Faldos looked up, eyes filled with dread.

"What is it, kid?" he asked, knowing he wouldn't like the answer.

"Graves' cable line. It's starting to come loose! The weld isn't holding, the whole harpoon gun is gonna come loose!"

Lok cursed. "How long?"

"Minutes at best. I can try to glue it, but it's not gonna buy much time. I'm sorry, Lok, I made the weld as best as I could but—"

"Shaddup. Ya did fine. The weld looked good, I saw it. We're using these in ways they never intended. We've done our best just...just let me think."

But in truth, he didn't really need time to think. Even his feral mind could see the obvious answer. He was out of weapons. They'd all been emptied onto the body of the Nulljaw. No more guns, no more missiles or rockets.

He had only one thing left to throw at the monster.

With feet made of kuron. Lok dragged himself to the helm of the *Hunt or Be Hunted II*. He laid hands on the comfortable apparatus, as familiar to him as any limb of his own body. He sat down in the chair.

He thought of the wreckage of the *Hunt or Be Hunted I*, swearing to never again lose something so helplessly. He thought of his skeptical purchase of the *Hunt or be Hunted II*. Thought of every job he strained to pull, adding, bit by bit, to the ship's armor and arsenal. Thought of his hunts with the ship, in Ochre Mist, on Talvak's three moons, along the Cosmic Current. He thought of beasts he would never have slain without the ship. And he thought most of the chair he sat in.

Slickmoles have muddy dens. Springhounds have mountaintop lairs. Leviathans have cosmic roosts. And Lok had the *Hunt or Be Hunted II*.

He punched the throttle, engaging the main thruster. "Pull Graves out. He's done all he can…"

Faldos blinked. "Lok?"

He sighed. Though he would never admit it to Sendro, times like these, he really did feel old. "…And get ready to abandon ship."

Faldos stared at him for far too long before nodding with understanding. "All right." He tapped away at his controller. Ahead, the small speck of the puppet flew away from the rocket.

Even as they drew closer to the Nulljaw, Lok could see the wire from one of the rockets trembling awkwardly. Without further fanfare, it snapped free, and the rocket tore off to the planet below. Lok didn't bother calling it back. It was almost empty anyway.

Emboldened, the Nulljaw redoubled its efforts and it started rising back out of the planet's gravity well. As soon as it noticed Lok's ship, it snapped its jaws eagerly. Another core would give it a new lease on life. It could retreat back to the cloud, heal its wounds, and rebuild its armor. Return even bigger.

"Go ahead and jump kid, before I really get up to speed."

"You sure?"

"Yeah. And thanks. You did good, Faldos."

The boy tried and failed to hide the proud smile that put on him. "Anytime, Lok."

He popped the hatch, crawled up to the satellite ring, then leaped off the ship. Lok stepped away from the helm briefly, picking around the room. He found the Twinshot; the boy must've retrieved it. Good kid. He placed it on his back along with the blastspear. He cracked open lockers and found there were only three items he really wished to bring. The first was the shadowstring case. The second was an illsur knife with a name carved into its hilt. He stuffed it into his belt. The third was a satchel he'd loaded up just in case something like this happened.

Ahead, the other rocket broke free, trailing after its brother. The Nulljaw gave a mighty shake of its unchained body, mouth gaping in victory.

Lok stepped forwards and threw the throttle of the *Hunt or be Hunted II* all the way down. He lurched back, weakened inertial dampeners struggling. The Nulljaw, wounded, burned, dwindling fuel, still tried to get out of the way. Lok twisted the helm of the *Hunt or Be Hunted II* one final time, burying the bow of the ship in the Nulljaw's throat.

The beast bit down, trying all its might to chew its way out of the situation.

"Enjoy the meal. Hope ya choke on it."

Lok turned from the helm, cracked the hatch, and jumped out onto the top deck. He grappled down to the bottom of the satellite ring, He hung on with one hand. He looked up to admire his starship one more time.

"You did good."

He let go.

The *Hunt or Be Hunted II* and the Nulljaw accelerated towards the planet below. Lok watched the Nulljaw desperately eat its way to the ship's core.

Down.

The bow went first, chewed up like it was foil.

Down.

Next, it tore its way through the middle decks of the ship, most of which it'd already ravaged.

Down.

The Nulljaw was met by the durable shell of the engineering room. This, its jagged teeth struggled to breach.

Down.

Finally, the shell cracked like an egg. At long last, the Nulljaw swallowed its fresh core.

There was a chance, even with all the weight it'd just taken on, as far as it'd fallen, that the Nulljaw might just be able to compensate with the new core and climb back out.

Lok never left anything to chance.

He tapped his cuffcomp, activating the bomb he'd placed on the core. It exploded, blowing out the rest of the Nulljaw's teeth.

Lok imagined the horror the Nulljaw felt. After the pain faded, the realization would set in. That now nothing could stop its orbital decay. That the weight of its own nigh-impenetrable kuron armor, combined with the ship it'd just eaten would drag it inescapably to its doom. If it'd given up on the core and broken free of the ship to start with, it might've stood a chance. But no longer.

Down.

The Nulljaw and the last shreds of the *Hunt or Be Hunted II* faded against the red backdrop of Scarlet Morn.

Maybe a minute later, maybe an hour, they landed.

A crater appeared, a pinprick impact point from which spread out a wave of red dust and rock dilating across the surface. Lok imagined the Nulljaw's insides turning to liquid, its plates sent flying kilometers away, no part of its body even remotely identifiable. It was a thought that almost made him smile. Almost.

"Quarry slain," he said quietly.

"Be honest, was that the worst hunt you've ever been on?"

Lok looked over his shoulder to see Faldos on his puppets' back. He drifted up to Lok and extended Grave's hand.

"Not even close," Lok took the puppet's hand. They started the long path rocketing back to Ruby Roost.

"Well it's the worst one I've been on," Faldos said. "I was in not one but two ships as they were being violently ripped apart. We had to fight off three rabid clutchers. We only escaped with the skin on our backs. And I'm gonna have to see those teeth in my nightmares." a smile crept into Faldos' voice. "I'll also keep seeing the Nulljaw make a crater in Scarlet Morn for a long time too. I guess technically this was also the best hunt I've ever been on."

"It grows on you." Lok said, rotating a shoulder. He was already feeling the aching in his bones from going Feral. It was going to be rough tomorrow. He touched the tooth at his belt. "Oh, and in case you want a keepsake, there's more teeth back there."

"Actually," From a compartment in Graves, Faldos withdrew a broken piece of a Nulljaw tooth. "I already got one. Pulled this out of our survey ship after the first attack. Funny how it feels different now."

"Before it was proof that you survived. Now it's proof you won."

Lok's cuff comp started ringing. He answered.

"You just had to wreck the station, didn't ya?" Vosta asked. Ruby Roost was still a ways off but the shredded bit of hull was just visible.

"I barely scratched it."

"I doubt the Burgrave will see it that way. But I'm guessing you at least slayed the beast, judging by the way you redecorated Scarlet Morn's face."

"Yeah, the beast is dead. And so is the Hunt or Be Hunted II."

"Oh, Lok. I'm sorry."

"It was just a ship."

She didn't call him on that. Even if they both knew it wasn't true.

"Well, on the bright side, five million crowns will give you plenty of options on buying a new one. On the downside I'm betting they'll want you to pay for some of that damage on Ruby Roost. Oh and I got some Gresknuk steaks waiting for you too."

"Attagirl. But first thing's first: I'd like to introduce you to someone."
He patched the three of them into a group frequency. "This is Faldos.
Son of an old buddy of mine. Faldos, this is Vosta. She finds me jobs."

"My pleasure, Vosta."

"Nice to meet you, Faldos. I apologize for the loveable bag of fur
that's been dragging you around."

"I think I've been doing the dragging."

"Well I'd love to stay and chat more but, I better go calm down the
Burgrave. I'll try to keep his claim for repairs under ten thousand. It
was nice to meet you Faldos and I think it's nice that Lok has someone else to watch his back in the wild."

She left those words hanging in the air. Ashing woman.

Lok cleared his throat. "She don't..." he didn't finish and tried
again. " I guess you'll be hopping on the first ferry out. Right?"

Faldos kept staring at the tooth. Eventually he spoke. "I'm...not
so sure about that."

Lok tilted his head in silent question.

Faldos was long in pushing the words out. "...The more time
I've spent around you, Lok, the more I think I didn't really know my
father that well."

"Oh?"

"As far as I can tell you knew him far better than I did. Saw what
kind of man he was before he had to settle down to take care of his
family. I'd like to know more about that man. I'd like to find out what
he saw in all this. But even beyond that I...I'd like to learn how you do
what you do. How you slay your fears so easily. Back there it was all I
could do to just react to things that were attacking me. And most of
that was behind the safety of a controller. But you dove in no matter
what, with no hesitation. I think if I could learn how to do that, I'd
be able to manage just about anything. I never did figure out what I
wanted to do with my life so..."

"So?"

He sighed with regret. "So, I think I'd like to stay on with you for
a while. If you'll have me."

"Well, kid, I haven't got much. In fact, just about everything I did own was back on that ship I just buried in the crust of Scarlet Morn. Getting a new one anywhere near as decent will take all the reward money from this job and half again to arm and fit it."

"And I suppose getting some decent gear of my own will cost a crown or two." Faldos sighed. "I don't even know where to start. "

"You've got a great start already: a real nice huntin' puppet."

"That's enough?"

"Only thing a hunter needs is a sharp knife and a good plan. Speaking of…" Lok removed another item from his belt and handed it to Faldos.

"What's this?" He asked, taking the knife.

"It was your dad's. Used that blade the whole time I knew him as a hunter. He gave it to me the day he quit. Figured it belongs to you now, if you're taking this path."

Faldos clenched a fist around the handle and drew the blade. It shone in the red reflection of the planet.

One day, there'd be a reckoning when Faldos' mother found out about this. Lok resolved to put off that conversation as long as possible.

"So," Faldos said. "Where to next? Hunt a Saurbane? A Trove Guardian?" His eyes gleamed with a mix of fear and excitement. "…a Leviathan?"

It was Lok's turn to laugh. "You just started and want to make history?"

"Not really. Just don't know what to expect."

"We'll start with something smaller. And hopefully in a place with more air. And gravity."

"Did it go this bad the first Hunt my dad went on?" Faldos asked.

"Oh much worse. We sorta broke a colonial city."

"What? How do you break a city?"

"It's a long story, and one for another time."

Faldos looked down at his father's knife. "You think he'd like that I'm doing this?"

"I think he'd be terrified…but yeah. He'd be excited to show you the ropes. I'll do my best in his place."

That made the kid smile. He looked down at the knife again and gave it a few test swings. His form would need work.

Lok would have to tell the kid someday soon, what really happened the day Runo died. The disaster that'd killed Faldos' father wasn't just some industrial accident, but the plot of a monster that'd hunted him across the stars.

But this was neither the time nor place for that discussion. He'd let this victory breathe in case Faldos changed his mind and left hunting behind after the thrill wore off. He owed the boy's mother that much.

"Hey, Lok?" Faldos said, cutting through his thoughts. "How long before the nightmares go away?"

"They never do."

The boy scowled, but Lok only smiled.

"You just learn to start slaying the monsters, even in the nightmares."

"*Hunters.*" Faldos shook his head. "Should I be worried that that almost made sense to me?"

Lok barked a laugh.

"It's 'cause you're one now, too, Faldos. Welcome to the Hunt."

# Afterword and Acknowledgements

Orbital Prey was not supposed to be my first book. That honor was supposed to belong to a story called One of the Strong. I languished writing and rewriting it for years but never quite got it to a position where I liked it enough to release it. Next I began work on a long term project called Starstrider. But Starstrider will be long in the making and I grew anxious to have something with my name on it, something I could publish. But I also wanted to keep my creative focus in that same setting. Orbital Prey was born.

I wear this book's inspiration on the sleeve, though I will not specifically name the certain shark film I borrow from. Also to thank for the book's concept, is an animated movie about sea monsters the latter half of which I found so disappointing I was inspired to write a story with the opposite conclusion.

Lok was easy to write, the overworked and underpaid elder hunter was partially based on an old boss of mine, while also adding bits of my own personality. I'd like to be half as cool as that old shadowy bag of fur someday.

Faldos was trickier. But for a character who was hard to nail down, a young man finding his place in the universe seems to have fit nicely. I'm not entirely comfortable with how similar I am to him. His journey into hunting, like my own into publishing, has just begun.

At the end of this I can say I wrote the kind of story I wanted to read. I hope you enjoyed it too.

Now it's time for me to thank people.

My father for instilling in me his taste in movies and a love for books by reading to me. My mother for supporting my creative side. My brother, Nate, for introducing me to many of my weirder inspirations and helping me to develop a critical lens. And where would I be without my dear sisters Abby and Rachel?

I will also thank my uncle John who fueled my hunger for sci fi at a young age from which I've never fully recovered. And my cousin Josh, who, whether he realizes it or not, got me to start writing in the first place.

I will further thank Simon, a constant writing partner and critic who shaped my own writing too greatly to quantify. And Josh who's cheered on this book and the greater universe it lives in since I first told him about it. Also, Kyla and Tyler for being beta readers.

And of course I thank everyone who worked on the production of this book, in particular cover artist Pantelis, and interior illustrator Inkerclark. Also concept art by Ahsan S., Gaston, and Gonzzart. The Hunt or Be Hunted II design by Greg. The map by Z Sajjad. Proofreads by Belle Manuel. And layout and formatting by Keven A. All can be found on Fiverr.

That's all, for now. Go slay your own fears.

www.ingramcontent.com/pod-product-compliance
Lightning Source LLC
Chambersburg PA
CBHW071108100726
47908CB00008B/2316